D1738232

CRISPIN AND THE GREAT TREE

CRISPIN AND THE GREAT TREE

The way up is the way down

P.S. Naumann

Illustrations by Jay Montgomery

Loyola Jesuit Residence
1419 Salt Springs Road
Syracuse, New York
1 3 2 1 4

This book was printed in the United States of America.

Cover and interior illustrations by Jay Montgomery © 2010
Cover design by Jay Montgomery
www.jaymontgomery.com

To order additional copies of this book, contact:
Xlibris Corporation
1-888-795-4274
www.Xlibris.com
Orders@Xlibris.com

65054

DEDICATION

For the greater glory of God certainly,
and for all those who read aloud to me,
all those to whom I read aloud,
and all those to whom I might have read aloud
had circumstances permitted.

WITH GREAT AND LASTING GRATITUDE

for Ronald and Donald and Moira and Dave,
for Gerald and Michael and all those who gave
me advice and support – my Province and friends
in the Jesuit Res. on whom one depends.
Above and before the unmentionable rest,
all of the Wegmans Writers West.

NOTE:

The Atlantic Archipelago,
fictitious setting of these books,
consists of seven islands ruled by Nine Houses or families.
The Archipelago lies in the mid-Atlantic
Somewhere not too far south of Iceland.
Like the Althing of Iceland,
The Archipelago has an Allgathering once a year.
At this, the heads of the Nine Houses, the bishops, and the abbots
meet to settle juridical matters and, rarely, to make a law binding on all.
In alphabetical order, the Nine Houses are as follows:
Falconstryke, Laggenhorst, Montalban, Rintoul, Skarpingdin,
Southlocke, Trefoil, Tryce, and Whithorn.

The Atlantic Archipelago disappears
When you close the covers of this book.

ONE

TO THE FOREST

Once upon a time, only the year before yesterday, there lived a boy named Crispin. He was a young boy, stout of heart and strong of limb, but just a little smaller than other boys his age.

One morning when Crispin was considerably older than five but not nearly so old as ten, he woke up and got out of bed very early. No one else was up, not on this particular morning. Even the sun was not up and the air was still chilly and moist. This was the day Crispin was going to climb the great pine tree, *his* tree. Of course it wasn't *really* his tree. It belonged in the forest where it stood, and his parents had warned him never to go into the forest. Nevertheless, that was where he was going. He knelt down at the edge of his bed. Perhaps because his head was so full of plans and possibilities, or perhaps because he was going to disobey his parents, or perhaps both, he got up again quite quickly.

He took off his pajamas and hung them in the closet, put on his underwear, a long sleeved shirt, sat down to pull on his knee socks and his corduroy knickers, and then thrust his feet into his hightops and started lacing them up. He had finished one and started the other when something occurred to him. The hightops had leather soles and, because leather was slippery in trees, could be dangerous. But they were the best thing for hiking, especially through tall grass and underbrush. What to do? If he wore his sneakers—best for climbing trees—and came back with tears and burdocks in his socks, there would be trouble.

His knapsack! The very thing! He finished the lacings with nimble fingers, pulled on a heavy, old blue sweater that was practically through in the elbows, and made sure he had his jackknife and a clean handkerchief in his back pocket. Then he dove into his closet and fished out the knapsack, and put his sneakers into it. He had decided not to wash his face since running water makes noise in the bowl and the pipes. He tiptoed down to the kitchen. He had no need to worry about the stone stairs in the tower creaking beneath his feet, but leather footfalls made a tapping noise on stone. He went down the stairs very carefully.

The kitchen was still dark so Crispin turned on the light over the sink. He had to put a foot up on the radiator under the sink in order to reach that high, but he managed. He poured himself a glass of milk and drank part of it, cut a thick slice of bread, buttered it heavily and spread marmalade on it. For lunch he made two peanut butter and jelly sandwiches in quick succession, wrapped each one in wax paper and put them into the knapsack along with a hard boiled egg (also wrapped) and an apple.

Oh rats! I forgot the canteen. Should he go without it? No. Peanut butter always made him thirsty and stuck to the inside of his mouth. So back up to his closet he went, as quietly and quickly as he could, took the canteen from the hook where it hung by its strap, and started back down. Because it had barely started to grow light outside, the stairs were still dark. The boy misjudged the number of stairs and stepped off the second-to-last. He was very surprised when the floor was not where he thought it should be, lost his balance but regained it without falling. However, the canteen went flying, bouncing down the stone passageway.

He froze. And listened: nothing. No sounds from above. Mercifully, the racket had been dulled somewhat by the canteen's canvas cover. He knew that if he had to tell his father or mother why he was up and what he was planning to do, he would not be allowed to do it. He picked up the canteen and went back into the kitchen, filled it from the pitcher of water in the refrigerator, refilled the pitcher and put it back. Then he repacked the knapsack, putting the heavy canteen and sneakers at the bottom and the lunch on top. He even remembered to put in a large paper napkin before he tied up the knapsack and put his arms through the straps. He finished the glass of milk, running water into the empty glass and leaving it in the sink, picked up his slice of bread, turned out the light and let himself out by the garden door. As he shut the door carefully and quietly behind him, he thought, *Great tree, get ready. Here I come!*

Taking the first bite out of the bread and butter and marmalade, he crossed the level terrace lawn and hurried down the steps into the garden. Crispin's house stood on the shoulder of a low hill, just where the road turned down toward the fringe of the wood. There was the narrow road, then a very high wall with a big arched gate through it, then a cobblestone yard and, across the yard, at the top of its big stone step, the wide front door of his house. The house was a very old, grey stone house. At one end stood a tower, a real tower, although not a very tall one, with the stone steps that went round and round inside and an outside door at the bottom. These were the stairs Crispin had gone down to the kitchen. On the other side of the house, opposite the courtyard, were the terrace lawn and the steps down into the garden. At the bottom of the garden was an orchard, and just beyond the orchard a meadow and then the woods. If you went deep enough into the woods you came to the forest. The boy had been into the woods many times. Once, with his older brother, he had even gone almost to the end of the woods. But, until today, he had never gone as far as the forest.

*

Crispin lived with his father and mother and his two brothers. His older brother (that was Tarquin) was not much older. His younger brother (Justin) was still a baby, barely beginning to learn to walk.

He moved silently down through the shadowy garden, hurrying to get out of range of his father's voice, so he could not be called back and asked where he was going. He finished the slice of bread, butter, and marmalade, and by the time he reached the end of the garden he had finished licking his fingers. As he passed the green bay tree that had been clipped carefully into a great round ball, he reached out and pulled off a leaf. The leaf was sticky to his fingers but he liked the smell of bay and held it up to his nose.

It was a simple matter to unlatch the gate through the garden hedge and close it behind him. By this time everything had begun to turn a luminous grey except the darker shapes of the orchard trees.

When he was younger, Crispin had started his tree-climbing escapades here in the orchard where the trees were easier to climb. But he soon discovered that the taller the tree, the higher he could climb, and the better he liked it. If they were very straight trees he could pretend that they were the masts of ships and he a sailor.

Once, from the very top of the big maple tree that shaded the terrace in summer, he had seen the next farm where the farmers lived who worked their own land as well as his father's. At first Crispin had been unable to climb it because he could not reach the lowest branch. But one day he had discovered a short ladder that had been left out in the orchard. He put it over his shoulder, carefully brought it through the gate, and leaned it up against the maple trunk on the side *away* from the house. It was just tall enough so that he could reach the bottom branch. Up he went, swung himself over that branch and started to climb. It was an easy climb, the branches were thick and close together and he got to the top quite handily. He had hardly been at the top a minute when he heard his mother calling.

"Crispin. Crispin."

Pause.

"Yes." He had tried to throw his voice so that it sounded as though it came from someplace else. It didn't work.

"Are you up in that tree?"

Another pause. He had already started scrambling down. "Yes."

"I want you to come down from there immediately, before you fall." By this time his mother was standing by the foot of the tree. "But come down carefully."

Crispin swung down from the lowest branch and dropped into the grass.

"Look at your hands and knees—they're filthy dirty."

He looked. They *were* pretty grim. "It'll wash off," he said.

"Well, do it immediately. And don't get your towel all dirty—make sure you wash it *all* off with soap and water first."

And he had barely had time to look around from the top of the maple tree. Well, today he would look out from the top of a much taller tree.

Through the orchard he went, across the meadow and, minutes later, he was well into the woods, familiar territory to himself and his brother Tarquin. Deeper and deeper into the woods he traveled, instinctively following almost invisible animal paths that led in the direction of the forest. The trees grew larger and taller and darker. Then, almost suddenly, the woods came to an end at a deep, swiftly flowing stream. He had not expected the stream, nor had he expected the bridge over it, a very old stone bridge that somebody had been keeping in excellent repair. It crossed the stream in a single, graceful arch.

Most amazing bridge, thought Crispin, and he started to cross. He had read about trolls in books and knew that they lived underneath bridges. But he was thinking about who might have built the bridge and how very lucky that whoever had built it had done so just here, where he wanted to cross the stream. So he ran up one side of the bridge and down the other. Even as the boy ran over the bridge he dropped the green bay leaf he was still carrying into the stream. That was the right thing to do.

Since there was a bridge, the path did not surprise him. It led gently upwards toward the shoulder of the first hill, taking occasional detours around the trunks of trees that grew larger and taller as the Indian scout (that Crispin had turned himself into) sped noiselessly on. Actually, his progress was not entirely noiseless because of the thud of the thick leather soles on his high tops, but the path was clean, almost as if it had been swept. The boy looked about him eagerly, trying to identify birds as they flashed past or sang from somewhere out of sight. The one thing that he didn't notice was that the branches of the trees began well above anything he could reach. He recognized the trees well enough, the oak and beech, pine and hemlock; their trunks were immensely tall and straight. There was something almost watchful and brooding about them that made Crispin pass among them as rapidly as possible. Then the sun came up and started to make horizontal shafts of light through the branches of the towering trees and he felt better, and safer.

The trees of the forest were so tall and Crispin so dwarfed among them that he could not see over them to the top of his great tree. But he had seen it from the window at the landing of the circular tower stairs outside his bedroom. That is where he had *first* seen it. From this window he could see down over the orchard to the woods and beyond, and over the woods to the forest which rose and fell on its hills and into its valleys as far as the eye could see. Across these valleys and not *too* far into the forest, the trees rose up a hill somewhat higher than the other hills around. On the top of that hill an enormous pine tree reared its bulk, towering well above any tree that Crispin could see (or even imagine) in any direction, no matter which way or out of which window he looked.

Some mornings, instead of getting dressed and having his breakfast as he should, the boy would stand on the landing and gaze across the valleys at the giant tree. He liked to think of the great distances a young boy could see from the top of that tree, and how one day he would set out and climb to the very top and look out. *I'll bet I could see practically the whole county.* He often dreamed of what it might look like. He thought he would even be able to see the city, Tryceholdings, where his father worked.

After every heavy storm that swept over their hollow valley, Crispin would climb the tower stairs to the landing and look anxiously out, making sure that the great pine tree had not been splintered by lightning. Sometimes during the winter he could not see the tree for days at a time because of the snow that whirled past the window. He would grow uneasy then and peer out into the pouring white until his eyes began to blur and grow tired. Once, after a particularly bad early spring rain, which had frozen as it fell, coating everything with a wrapping of ice, the westering sun had flashed a beam into the glazed branches of the great tree, sending a blaze of light that had shone out to Crispin. It had seemed like a personal signal from the tree to say, "See, I am still here; I am still standing; I am still waiting for you."

This was the day he was going to keep that appointment. Now he relied on the path he was following because it was the only path; it seemed to be going in the right direction, and it had grown broader. Then came the first set of steps. Just where the path began to grow somewhat steep, someone had constructed a broad flight of steps! Perhaps the same person who had built the bridge? Made out of large rectangular stones they were, carefully fitted together and well-worn, the sort of steps at the top of which you would expect to find a castle door. There was no castle door, just the path again, gently rising and rounding another big tree and turning into another flight of steps, even broader then the first.

Crispin hurried on, wondering mightily about the steps and where they might be leading, and to what? His heart began to beat faster, perhaps because he felt he must be getting closer, or maybe just because he was climbing so many steps in such a hurry. At last the path rounded an enormous rock, very tall, almost like a sentinel. There was a final, gentle flight of even broader steps that led up to a huge, round, earthen platform which rose ever so slightly to form the hilltop. At the top of the rise—was *his* tree! His great tree, more magnificent than he had dreamed! His throat knotted and tears, just two, filled the corners of his eyes. He ran up the last, broad flight of steps and on up the final, gentle rise, his feet slipping because of the leather soles on the brown pine needles. There he stood among the gigantic roots, stretched out his hands to the trunk and leaned against it with his head between his arms. Breathing heavily from his final run, he took a step forward and leaned his forehead against the bark. It was practically an act of worship.

TWO

THE WOLF

The sun continued to rise and a ray, turned on and off by an intervening branch, tapped Crispin on the shoulder. Now to climb! What he had come for. He stepped back and looked up. The trunk of the great tree was very, very large around and the lowest branch was much too high for Crispin to reach. He had never thought of that! It was *his* tree, he had always been sure he could climb it, always. It had been waiting for him. And now? Not this! Perhaps, the other side? At that moment, from the other side of the tree, he heard the sound of chopping wood. He scrambled out from among the roots and hurried around the tree.

There he came upon a great, grey wolf. With a giant ax the wolf was chopping dead sticks and branches that had fallen out of the tree. Nearby, from a tripod, a cauldron hung on a large chain. Under the cauldron stood a teepee-like arrangement of sticks and twigs, and little tongues of flame already flickered up through the sticks and licked the bottom of the great pot. Faint wisps of smoke carried off downwind. The wolf's back was to Crispin.

"Excuse me, sir," said Crispin, who had been taught to be very polite.

"In a moment, young man," said the wolf, without turning around.

Crispin had never seen a live wolf before. Indeed, he had never seen such a big dog. He certainly had not seen one chopping wood, nor had he really expected it to talk.

"Now then," said the wolf, turning around and looking at Crispin narrowly, "what can I do for you?"

"I'm going to climb this tree, but I'm . . ." Crispin hesitated, " . . . but I'm too short to reach the lowest branch."

"And you want me to give you a leg up, is that it?"

"Yes, please, if you would be so kind, as soon as I change into my sneakers."

"But, of course. Nothing could be simpler. Just let me add this wood to the fire." The wolf made a bundle of the sticks and twigs and carried them over to where the great cauldron hung over the flickering fire. The wolf gingerly increased the size and height of the teepee of twigs and then, crouching down on all fours, he blew gently but steadily at the base of the fire. The flames began to lick up higher. A burning twig snapped, and then another, until there was quite a crackle and blaze. Then the wolf stood up and removed the large cover from the cauldron and looked in.

While the wolf was coaxing his fire, the boy unlaced his high tops and changed into his sneakers, pulling the laces tight and double-tying them so that no long loops hung down.

"You don't mind if I leave my high tops here until I come down?" asked Crispin.

"Not at all; they will be perfectly safe."

"What are you going to cook in such a large pot?"

"Funny you should ask," replied the wolf. "I cook whatever comes to hand." And then, replacing the cover, he said, "I'll take the cover off once the water begins to boil."

"Watch out for your spoon!" exclaimed Crispin, pointing to the handle of a very large iron spoon that lay dangerously near the increasing fire. The wolf snatched up the spoon and placed it at a good distance from the fire, between two cans, labeled SALT and PEPPER.

"Well, then," said the wolf, "one good turn deserves another," and he walked over to the trunk of the massive pine and, putting his back against it, made a cup with his paws. "Elevator going up," he said. Crispin put his right foot in the cup and buried his fingers in the grey fur of the wolf's shoulders to steady himself. The wolf began to lift gently and straighten up and, as he did so, Crispin looked deep into his eyes.

"You have yellow eyes," said Crispin as he rose past the wolf's head.

"Do I?" said the wolf, who had never really looked at himself before. "It must be from the fires inside."

With the wolf's help Crispin rose slowly to the lowest branch, but the branch was so huge and still so high that Crispin could not climb onto it nor get his arms around it. So the wolf walked carefully forward several paces from the main trunk to where the branch sagged a bit under its own weight. There it began to divide into smaller branches, and Crispin could let go, straighten up, and swing himself into the tree. He faced himself around towards the trunk and saw that the branch ahead of him was broader than the path he had first taken through the forest. He looked down to the wolf below him. The wolf appeared smaller than when Crispin was standing next to him on the ground. There he had looked very large indeed.

"Thank you very much, sir, for your help."

"Remember, what goes up must come down," replied the wolf.

Crispin stood erect and sprang lightly up the broad branch ahead of him.

"Stop!" cried the wolf.

Crispin stopped.

"Don't you want an enchantment?"

"A what?" asked Crispin, who was not sure what the wolf had in mind.

"An enchantment: something to help you on your way."

"Is that like . . . magic?" asked Crispin.

"Yes, you *could* say that," replied the wolf. "I don't think you would be too far wrong if you said that. But, mind, there *is* a difference."

"Do you mean like a magic cap or a ring or a charm of words?"

"Yes, I suppose that's the idea."

"What is it?"

"Here." And the wolf bent over between two very large roots of the tree and passed up to Crispin a gentleman's big, green umbrella, rolled up tightly and snapped, with a handle of horn that hooked over your arm when you were doing something else, like fishing in your pocket for change or reading a newspaper. The umbrella was more than half the size of the boy himself.

"Thank you very much," said Crispin doubtfully, taking hold of the handle. "I've never heard of an enchanted umbrella before. Do you really think I'll need it?"

"You never know," said the wolf.

"What's it good for?"

"You never know," said the wolf.

"It won't fit in my knapsack."

"No. It wouldn't do much good there, anyway."

"Well, I think I'd better be going now."

"Hurry back down," said the wolf.

Crispin felt that he had spent quite enough time talking to the wolf and that meanwhile the sun had been getting higher and higher. He turned to his climb with excitement and determination and began to go up, resolutely, from branch to branch. The branches were very large and quite close together, so much so that it reminded him a little bit of climbing the tower stairs. He circled the trunk more than once. At first the umbrella got in his way and slowed his progress so that he was tempted to leave it hanging on a branch. He did not. He grew accustomed to having it with him and learned to manage it with some dexterity. At times it came in quite handy. He could use the handle to hook around a smaller branch and steady himself while he glanced about. It was almost like hanging onto the strap in a trolley car, although he was far too short to be able to reach that high.

For a while he could hear the wolf chopping at what sounded like larger branches, and every once in a while he caught just a trace of the smell of wood smoke. But the day was fine, the breeze was fresh, the pine filled his nostrils, and it wasn't long before Crispin forgot all about the wolf and his ax. He also forgot about the cauldron.

THREE

TROUBLE ABOVE

The boy was making steady progress up the great tree, but gradually became aware of two things: the first was that there didn't seem to be any birds about, as there had been earlier, and no squirrels either. He heard no songs or chattering, no cries or scolding, no drumming of woodpeckers on dead branches or stumps. *Can this tree be so large that nothing will come into it? No, that's silly. And, anyway, I'm in it.* So he kept on climbing.

The second thing Crispin became aware of was that there was someone, or some*thing*, somewhere in the tree above him. He thought he could hear something like humming. He looked up but could see nothing and continued to climb, although more warily. Then, suddenly, he heard a voice from above him.

"You: boy! Bring that umbrella up here."

It was the voice of a woman, an old woman, Crispin supposed, because it was cracked around the edges. *Funny* he thought, *how could she get way up here? And how **did** she know I had an umbrella? And she didn't say 'please'.* As yet he could see no one so he continued to climb and finally he paused, looked up, and saw a face looking down at him over the edge of a large limb. It *was* an old woman's face with a hooked nose, pointed chin and sharp, beady eyes. The face gave him a funny feeling in the pit of his stomach, an unpleasant feeling, and he stopped climbing just a branch or two below her

"That's right, boy, just pass that umbrella right on up to me. You can't come up any higher unless you give me your umbrella."

"But it's not mine to give away. It's on loan. The wolf at the bottom of the tree loaned it to me, and . . ."

"I know, I know, just hand it over . . . there's a good boy. You see, I'm an old woman who needs this umbrella, so do be a nice little boy and let me have it. I have great difficulty getting around."

Crispin, who greatly disliked being called a "little boy," objected: "If you have so much difficulty getting around, I really don't see how you could climb so high up this tree."

"Oooooooh, isn't he a clever boy, *my* my my my! Now lovey, clever little boy that you are, do give me the umbrella like a nice little boy, and then you can climb as high as you like. Or as high as you *can*," and the old woman snickered to herself.

"I'm *not* a 'little boy'," said Crispin, angrily, "and you certainly don't need the umbrella if you're climbing around in this tree. I can't imagine *how* you got up here in the first place."

"If you must know, I ran into the tree in the morning fog." And indeed, Crispin could see that the peak of her hat was crumpled and bent. "And I need the umbrella to help me retrieve my broomstick."

"Only witches ride on broomsticks." Crispin's eyes widened and then narrowed thoughtfully.

"Ah! The coin drops," said the witch sarcastically.

"Perhaps if you let me climb up there I can retrieve your broomstick for you. Where is it?"

"No, no . . . . none of that! It's the umbrella I want and I begin to grow impatient. You go no higher unless I get the umbrella first. Be quick, before I try a spell or two."

Now Crispin was still young enough so that he had not yet learned to be afraid of much of anything. On the other hand, he had heard from the Brothers Grimm (which his mother had read to him and which he now read for himself) that witches were not particularly nice and couldn't be trusted. And they knew about enchantments. It seemed clear that this one knew something about the umbrella and that she was not about to impart any secrets to him. Then again, on the *other* other hand, perhaps she was bluffing about not letting him pass and her bluff could be called.

Crispin fixed the handle of the umbrella under the flap of his knapsack and secured it with the rawhide tie. It hung down somewhat awkwardly in back but it freed both his hands. He climbed up a branch or two and reached up, putting both hands on the branch where the witch was standing.

"Oh no you don't!" cried the witch, and she trampled on the backs of his hands and fingers, grinding them under her heels. Crispin snatched his hands away so quickly that he almost lost his balance and toppled over backwards. Despite the pains in his hands he had to grab onto whatever he could to keep himself from falling. She *hadn't* been bluffing.

Crispin sat on a large branch and pondered. The fingers on both hands burned and tingled and he put them gently under his armpits until they began to feel better. Then he inspected the damage. One of his fingers was turning blue and he sucked a little blood off one of his fingernails. His hands had grown dirty from the climb and were sticky with pine pitch, but nothing seemed broken, just sore. He looked up to where he could just see the witch's shoes and ankles. She was standing on the broad branch above his head with her back pressed tight against the trunk of the tree. He could see the buckles on her shoes glitter beneath their grime. He could see her red and white striped stockings sag about her bony ankles. And he could see where the hem of her petticoat had been ripped and hung down below her skirt.

"I give you one more chance, witch," he said, with new energy in his voice, "will you let me climb up this tree, or must I do something drastic?" And he unlaced the umbrella from his knapsack.

"Hee hee hee," cackled the witch. "What a determined little boy he is! Threats, idle threats, will get you no place, my boy, least of all up this tree. I am still above you, don't you see, and I will stamp on your fingers with my heels, and step on your head with my feet. So just give me the enchanted umbrella . . . . drat!" And she covered her mouth quickly with both hands because she had said too much, too angrily, without thinking.

Just at that moment, when both hands were over her mouth and not holding on to the tree, Crispin reached up with the umbrella, hooked the handle around one of the witch's ankles, and gave a mighty tug. The witch teetered for a moment on one foot, hopped along the branch, struggling to regain her balance, her hands clutching wildly at nearby branches to steady herself. But there were no branches near enough. With a piercing shriek she plunged forward and fell head over heels down through the unresisting branches of the great tree.

Crispin listened closely and heard, with satisfaction, the faint sound of a splash as the witch dropped right into the wolf's cauldron. Then all was still.

Suddenly all the birds started singing. A jubilant racket arose as well from some crows and from a family of squirrels that threw down a shower of pine cones in the direction the witch had taken.

"I wasn't as little as she thought," Crispin announced to the rejoicing birds, and he started to climb upwards again, onto the branch where the witch had stood, and then on to the next. Then he stopped. The broomstick. There it lay, far out at the end of a spreading branch. It had not been dislodged by the witch's fall. In fact, it was on an entirely different branch. Otherwise, she might have grabbed it as she fell past and then what would have happened?

"If I can reach it, the broom is mine," thought Crispin, "and it must be a magic broom if the witch could fly around on it. Or maybe it's an evil broom and should be destroyed." Since he was smaller and younger and lighter than the witch, he could crawl out much further on the branch than she had been able to, had she tried, and he could get much closer to the broomstick. But the closer he came the more the branch began to sag and the more danger there was that the broom would drop off . . . . or that the branch would break. The knapsack! He squirreled his way back up the branch, took off his knapsack and his heavy sweater too, and tried again. Oh so carefully, he reached out with the handle of the umbrella, hoping to hook it around the broomstick and draw it to himself. He hooked it. And pulled gently: and again. The broom shifted, the heavy end went down, making the broom stand upright, and drop from sight.

Crispin had all he could do to get back up the branch to safety. *Oh well,* he thought, *perhaps the wolf would know what to do with it. Perhaps he would break it over his knee or give it a chop with his ax and throw the pieces onto his fire.* At that moment there came a terrific **BANG** and a puff of acrid, black smoke drifted away on the breeze. Then the great tree itself seemed to stand a little taller and a little straighter than it had before. *So much for the broomstick,* thought the boy.

Since the day was growing warm, he decided to leave his sweater behind and pick it up on the way down. He would be more comfortable without it and little twigs and pine needles would not get caught in his shirt as they did in the sweater.

So he started to climb again. And he thought as he went up, *I hope the wolf wasn't hurt by the explosion.*

FOUR

AN ALARMING LUNCH

Crispin felt that he had been making considerable progress and that perhaps he ought to rest and look about a bit. So he straddled a big branch and put his back against the trunk. But the knapsack got in the way, making his back uncomfortable. He eased himself out of the shoulder straps, shifting the umbrella from one hand to the other as he did so. Then he stood up and hung the umbrella on a branch above his head and hung the knapsack over the dead stump of a branch just a bit to one side. Again, he settled himself comfortably against the great tree trunk and looked out.

At this height the branches had become shorter. They were still almost as big as pathways leading away from the tree trunk, but he could see out more easily. There wasn't much to see except the nearby trees. Crispin was close to reaching the top of those, but not there yet. He leaned out and glanced up to see what he could see of the sky. Some small clouds drifted along here and there but the day was bright and the sun warm. As he relaxed against the friendly tree trunk his eyelids grew heavy. So he closed them . . . . and slept.

Crispin awoke with a start. How long had he been asleep? He dug into the corners of his eyes with his fists to clear away the fuzzy spots before them. But the more he dug, and the more he blinked, the more the spots resolved themselves . . . into a leopard, a rather large leopard, staring at him from only a few feet away. It was crouched on the very branch on which he was sitting, and its muscles quivered under its coat as though it was ready to spring.

"Hello," said Crispin, controlling his alarm, "it's a leopard, isn't it?"

"Hello," said the leopard, "it's a small boy, and a very hungry leopard." And with that it made a purring snarl from the back of its throat and bared all of its sharp teeth. Meanwhile, the sky had begun to grow very dark and thunder growled at the same time as the leopard, so that Crispin was not quite sure which was which. The leopard tensed its muscles again.

"Wait a minute, you can't eat me!" the boy exclaimed.

"Why ever not?" growled the leopard *and* the thunder, both of which were drawing nearer.

"Because I'm not as small as I look," said Crispin indignantly, "and because I have to climb to the top of this tree, and, anyway, I don't think my father and mother would like it; not at all. And it's about to rain cats and dogs, if you'll pardon the expression." And with that Crispin reached up, took down the big green umbrella, opened it up and held it, as a defense, between himself and the leopard.

"Good heavens! He has disappeared!" cried the leopard, who had never seen an umbrella before.

At that very moment big drops of rain began to spatter down through the tree, splintering into finer drops as they came through the pine needles. Then lightning flashed and thunder roared and the leopard snarled in frustration because the small boy had vanished and the rain drops were beginning to run down its nose. Crispin, who had begun to get wet himself, automatically raised the umbrella over his head to keep the rain off.

"My word, here is the boy again with an amazing device for keeping dry," said the leopard, startled. "Do you have room under that thing for a leopard who is just the teensiest bit bigger than you are? I don't like getting wet any more than you do."

Crispin saw that it was going to rain even harder. He looked at the leopard who was ruffling its coat to keep the rain off and who looked very depressed.

"Do you promise to behave yourself if I let you under this umbrella?" asked Crispin, who felt sorry for the beast.

"Yes, yes, of course."

"Cross your heart and hope to die?"

"Cross my heart and hope to die, whatever *that* means," and the leopard crossed its heart with its right front paw.

"A promise is a promise," said Crispin, and he edged out onto the branch so that he could sit with both feet down one side, and he held the umbrella up higher. Giving a mighty shake to its coat, the leopard sprang under the umbrella and sat close up to Crispin. The heavens opened and the rain poured down in great sheets as the lightning flashed and the thunder rolled and the tree quivered ever so slightly.

"What a marvelous invention," shouted the leopard above the noise of the thunder. "Wherever did you get it?"

"From the wolf at the bottom of the tree," shouted back Crispin. "He says it is an enchantment but I can't figure that out. It seems just an ordinary umbrella to me."

"To me it seems very wonderful indeed, and I should like to have one for my *very* own. I am continually outside in the rain and snow and suffer terribly from colds and ague as a consequence."

"Perhaps I'll give you this one when I get down out of this tree. If the wolf does not want it back again," said the boy, who had begun to think ahead.

"Oh, wolves," said the big cat, "they're just another kind of greedy dog. I shouldn't worry about the wolf if I were you." And the leopard narrowed its eyes to very slits, as cats will do, and made a menacing purr in the back of its throat. But the leopard, for all its subtlety, was not thinking ahead, probably because it was a leopard and not a threatened, small boy.

Eventually, with the steady drumming of the rain on the umbrella, and with the warmth and the softness of the leopard's coat, he began to feel drowsy again. As his eyes closed, the umbrella began to sag from its upright position until finally the leopard took it gently in its own paw and Crispin rested his cheek against the leopard's shoulder and slept again.

The rain continued to drum steadily on the umbrella. Then it began to slack off . . . and finally stopped entirely. The sun came out and a thousand thousand droplets glistened on the pine needles as Crispin woke up.

The leopard surrendered the umbrella reluctantly when the boy took it back. "Thank you for holding it. I guess I dropped off." He closed it (*Now I see how it works,* thought the leopard), hung it again on its branch, and looked up. "Oh, leopard, how beautiful the tree is! See the sun sparkle through all these drops."

"It's damp." And as if to confirm that, a little breath of a breeze sent a shower of water crystals onto them both. The boy shook his head and the animal its coat.

"It certainly must be lunch time by now," said Crispin. "I'm hungry."

"That makes two of us, but I'm afraid only one of us will eat." Once again the leopard growled a snickering snarl and crouched, tensing its muscles to spring.

"But not me!" gasped Crispin.

"You're all I've got," whispered the leopard through clenched teeth.

"But we've sheltered under the same umbrella. And you crossed your heart and promised."

"A leopard *must* eat," said the leopard.

"If you wanted something to eat, why didn't you eat that witch earlier?"

"Which witch?"

"The one down below that gave me all that trouble about the umbrella. I think she dropped into the wolf's kettle." Crispin had been inching backwards along the damp branch but now his back was against the trunk of the great tree and there was nowhere else to go, except down.

"Why didn't *you* eat her? What do boys eat, anyway?" The leopard carefully avoided the word *little* and purred soothingly in the back of its throat. Slowly it put out a paw to advance.

"I'm glad you asked that question. I have almost forgotten my egg and my apple. I don't suppose you've ever had a peanut butter and jelly sandwich?" Crispin tried anything to gain a little time.

"I've never even *heard* of a peanut butter and jelly sandwich. What is one? Something to eat, or something to wear . . . or what? Something to eat I *do* hope, for your sake," muttered the leopard. It gazed steadily at the boy who appeared to be growing fatter and larger and more appetizing by the second.

"Something very good to eat," said Crispin reaching for his very damp knapsack. He soon had it undone and the contents spread out on the branch before him. The wax paper he put back into the knapsack. "This is the hard boiled egg, and these the peanut butter and jelly sandwiches, and this is the apple. It's not much but it's what I brought. I wasn't expecting company. The hard boiled egg is much better with a little mustard." He said this in the hope that the leopard would decline the egg. "Would you like to try half?"

"I think I'll try the whole thing," said the leopard, leaning forward with a look of anticipation on its face. Suddenly the egg was gone. "An appetizer," said the leopard, looking pleased with itself.

"Well, you don't have to be so greedy. You remind me of my brother, the older one."

"Is he around here someplace?" The leopard looked down the tree as far as it could see and then up into the branches above. "I can't see him and don't smell him." And, snap! The apple disappeared as quickly as the egg.

"He's not part of this expedition," said Crispin. "Here, have a sandwich." He picked one up and held it out carefully towards the leopard, with his fingers as much out of the way as he could manage. He was afraid that if he just let the leopard help itself it would take both at once and he wouldn't have anything at all to eat.

"The apple was lovely and sweet," said the leopard, "like sherbet after the fish." It leaned towards the sandwich and took the whole thing at once and began chewing while Crispin picked up the other and took a big bite. He ate quickly to make sure he got *some*thing.

"Thrick! It's a thrick! It makes my jaws sthick together!" Not speaking too plainly, the leopard wasn't. "You thricked me," and the leopard tried to clean off its teeth as best it could with its tongue, alternately swallowing and cleaning. "Mmmmmmm, but it is tasty. Do you have anything to drink?"

"Just the water in my canteen . . . . and that's probably pretty warm by now."

"Warmth doesn't matter as long as it's wet."

Crispin fished the canteen out of his knapsack, hung the knapsack back on the branch, and unscrewed the top of the canteen. He held it up to his mouth with both hands, and took several swallows, showing the leopard how it was done.

The leopard held the canteen up high before its open mouth, the water gurgled out with a rush and hit the back of the leopard's throat. The poor beast coughed and spluttered, choked and gasped and before he knew what he was doing, Crispin was pounding it on the back. The leopard gave a mighty coughing sneeze and its eyes filled with tears. Then it cleared its throat from as far back as it could start, and put its head down between its paws.

"No napkins?" The leopard dried the corners of its eyes with its paws, cleared its throat again, and subsided onto the limb. "No napkins." Sniff.

"Actually, there is," said Crispin, "just one big paper one, but you're welcome to that."

"Linen's the only thing." And the leopard sniffed again, took the paper napkin that Crispin held out to it, blew its nose somewhat noisily and sat back on its haunches.

"Meanwhile, what has become of my canteen?"

"Darn the invention! It nearly did me in."

"Well it does no good to complain about things when you don't know how to use them. Can it have fallen all the way to the bottom of the tree? I don't see it anywhere."

"It hasn't fallen at all," said the leopard, "it has flown upward—like sparks, and something else . . . I forget what." And then the leopard stood up on its hind legs and stretched up into the branch above them and took the canteen gingerly in its jaws and shook it. The remaining drops of water flew out, the leopard dropped back onto all fours and presented the canteen to Crispin.

"Thank you very much," said the boy, wishing there were still some water left. "At least it will be lighter to carry. I wish we still had the apple. I was going to cut it in two with my knife. Like the egg."

"Irony!" exclaimed the leopard. "You're too young; it will get you no place."

"What is *irony*, please?" asked Crispin, who liked the sound of new words.

"It's . . . well, it's . . . it's the splice of life, that's what it is. As the man said."

"I thought that was *variety*."

"Splice, splice," growled the leopard. "Variety is the *spice* of life. Or so they say."

Crispin knew what *splice* meant because he had watched his father splicing the hammock ropes around the two trees that stood just the right distance apart on the lawn. But what that complicated maneuver with rope had to do with life was more than he understood, at the moment.

"May I ask another question?" And before the leopard could answer, Crispin went right on, "What are you doing up in this tree, anyway? I mean, I never expected to meet a leopard up here. If I had, I might never have come." He instantly regretted adding that last bit but it was too late. The leopard chose to ignore it.

"Well, I must admit, I was very surprised myself. You see, for a long time I have been helping to hold up a big, granite shield on the top of the county seat in Tryceholdings. You know, the county seat was formerly the castle of the Tryce family. The shield was their coat of arms held up on either side by heraldic beasts. How my husband and I qualify as heraldic beasts I have no idea, but there we are, or *were* until one morning, *this* morning, I believe, a voice said, 'Come along, you're needed.' So I sprang down and landed in this tree. I can't imagine how it worked and, unfortunately, I can't imagine how I'm supposed to get back . . . . or whether. I'm afraid my husband may be getting tired of holding up that coat of arms all by himself. And what was I needed for, anyway? Unless . . ."

The leopard sounded sad and disgruntled and, without thinking, Crispin reached out and scratched her head as he did with Magwitch, their old cat at home. "This needs thinking about," he said, knitting his brows and continuing to scratch behind the leopard's ears.

"Wait a minute! This umbrella is an enchantment, or so the wolf said who loaned it to me." Crispin took down the green umbrella from where he had hung it on a branch above him after the rain had stopped. "I wonder how it works, and what it does." He examined it carefully from one end to the other but there were no inscriptions or directions or clues. It was just a large, dark green umbrella. Then he opened it.

"Splendid invention! There's nothing like that on my castle roof." Again the leopard looked at the umbrella with considerable longing. "May I try holding it again?"

"Well, I don't see why not." He handed the umbrella to the leopard who sat on the branch holding it above her head like a summer parasol and looking rather smug. Crispin looked at the big cat reflectively and then a thought struck him.

"You know, the witch that I met down below wanted this umbrella in the worst way. She said at her age she had difficulty getting about and that it would come in very handy. I wonder . . . What did that voice say when you jumped off the courthouse roof?"

"Come along, you're needed."

"Right. Just hang on to that while I try something." Crispin did not want to lose the umbrella. On the other hand, he had no idea how it worked, or whether it worked, or when and where it would work, if it did, so he put his back against the tree trunk and said, in his deepest voice, "Go along! You're no longer needed!"

The leopard was gone. Completely. She had disappeared. The umbrella remained suspended in midair for a split second and Crispin grabbed it before it fell. His hands shook as he carefully collapsed the umbrella and hooked it over its branch above. Then he looked over the edge of the branch as far down the tree as he could see. No, no leopard and no trick. It couldn't be more gone. He hoped that somewhere in Tryceholdings was the courthouse that had just regained a leopard on its roof.

But, he thought, *the castle leopards . . . are stone.*

Looking up the tree Crispin could not yet see the top. The sun had already passed its zenith. The umbrella hung securely on its branch and the knapsack was empty except for the empty canteen. He would have to leave them both behind if he was going to achieve the top. Once again he started climbing. He could collect the knapsack and the umbrella on his way down.

FIVE

ONWARD AND UPWARD

It wasn't long before the branches began to grow shorter, and then Crispin noticed that he could now get his arms around the trunk itself. He had been concentrating so thoroughly on climbing that he had paid attention to little else, only trunk and branches. Once or twice he had almost run out of branches and then he had had to stretch up with both hands, pull himself up, swing a knee over the branch and then swing himself over. Then, quite unexpectedly, he realized just where he was. He was enormously high up and there seemed to be nothing around him but empty air. He felt a hollow feeling in the back of his knees and down his calves and the skin on the top of his head tightened. He held onto the trunk for dear life for fear he would grow dizzy and fall, and he shut his eyes until the empty feeling between his shoulder blades passed. He wondered whether he would ever be able to move again. However, with his cheek pressed tight against the tree, and his arms still wound around the trunk, he opened his eyes.

"Holy casmittima! I can see the whole world, practically!" At this height he knew that there could not be too much tree left above him, but he couldn't bring himself to bend even his head backwards and look up.

The next nearest branch above Crispin was a dead one. He could see the brown-needled, twiggy end of it without raising his head. Then he became aware, instinctively, that there was something, a bird, sitting on the branch, just out of sight. By holding on extra tight and very carefully tilting his head, he could just see it out of the corner of his eye. It was . . . Crispin tried to remember sitting with his father, looking through the plates in the bird book. It was . . . a peregrine. He thought he had seen a live one once before, soaring, but it was so high in the sunlight that he hadn't been sure. Now he blinked his eyes just to make sure it was really there. It was. And he stared at it, barely allowing himself to breathe.

"You might say 'Hello.'" This, in a high, nasal, razor-like voice.

Crispin swallowed the lump in his throat and whispered, hoarsely, "Hello. I was afraid I'd scare you away."

"We are not so easily put off our perch. And *you* seem to be the one who is frightened. This is the best perch in the county and I would hate to see it broken off beneath your weight."

"I don't think I'd like to break it off."

"No, I suppose not."

"I've never been up this high in a tree before." Crispin felt much safer looking at the falcon than at the empty space beneath him.

"Well, it *is* the tallest tree I know of anywhere. Frankly, I'm surprised you've come this far. I've been watching you for some time . . . . You certainly got rid of that witch easily enough."

"She made me angry," Crispin explained. "I get mean when I'm angry, I'm afraid. I'm not sure I should have done that."

"Have no regrets," counseled the peregrine. "She had been a menace for years. No one that I know will miss her. Then you shared, or *tried* to share, your lunch with the leopard. That was both wise and kind."

"More like *survival*, I thought."

"And you discovered the secret of the umbrella in practically no time at all. I thought you might quit while you were ahead. Climbing all the way to the top, are you?"

"That was my plan. But I'm having second thoughts. Being up this high takes some getting used to. I can see the top of this tree from my house, and I wanted to climb up and see my house from the top. But now my house is on the other side of the trunk and I'm not at all sure I want to lean out and take a look." Crispin was still very much aware of the great gap of space all around him, and he could still feel some of the empty feeling at the back of his knees.

"Oh look here, that branch you're sitting on is solid enough; even the woodpeckers don't go near it. Of course, they wouldn't, not with me sitting here. And the tree trunk isn't going to snap in two. What could be safer?" And the peregrine ruffled and then smoothed his feathers. "Which house is yours?"

"The big stone farmhouse; the one with the tower."

"Ah! I see, yes. I was ghosting over it earlier. Your cat doesn't keep the place up the way it used to."

"No, Magwitch is old and slow and doesn't do much anymore but sit in the sun and sleep."

"That's a help to me, of course; the mice from the barn aren't as lean and swift as they used to be. There's good hunting there these days."

"It must be lovely to fly, and plunge down as you do."

"Any raptor in flight is usually hard at work."

" . . . Then I could get home easily, and see everything from above, and sit up here like you."

"You're hardly equipped to fly, although there *was* one person once (or was it *two*?) . . . I remember my great-uncle telling me about him when I was a youngster. Trying to escape from some island . . . ."

"Icarus!" burst out Crispin, who had *The Wonder Book of Myths and Legends* on his shelf.

"What I was just about to say," said the peregrine, looking disgruntled, "from Crete in the Mediterranean. Confused his own apogee with the sun's zenith, if I remember correctly, and consequently came to grief."

"*Apogee*? Is that anything like *irony*?" Crispin was thinking of the leopard.

"Highest point in the flight, the arc, or the orbit, I think."

Crispin's conversation with the peregrine took his mind off his precarious seat and gradually he felt more at ease. Very, very, oh so slowly, he eased himself around so that he could look out on the other side of the trunk. There it was—the house and tower, courtyard, barn and sheds, the terrace lawn, gardens, orchard—it was all there. It all looked small and very far away; even the big maple and the oak had shrunk. To the boy there appeared to be a great deal more forest between himself and home than there was when looking in this direction from the tower window. Then he remembered that he was not supposed to have entered the forest at all. This was his first disobedience of any importance and there was so much forest still to return through. In the westering sun his home looked strangely quiet to Crispin.

"There's nobody there," he breathed.

"There was plenty of activity earlier. People were moving around all over the place: your father and mother and older brother, the farmers, too, as though they had lost something; or were looking for someone." The peregrine glanced shrewdly at Crispin.

"They were looking for me," said the boy quietly. "I'd better be getting back. It's beginning to get late, too."

"Don't they know where you are?"

"No. I left home before the sun was up and didn't tell anybody where I was going. Not even Tarquin."

"Tarquin?"

He's my older brother." Crispin was already down two branches.

"You're the middle brother, then?"

"Yes, Crispin. The baby is Justin."

"I'll remember *Crispin*."

"I'm sorry, I should have introduced myself earlier. Do peregrines have names?"

"Indeed we do. Mine is Malgrin. With a broad *a*; it rhymes with *awl*: Malgrin."

"Malgrin: I like that. You could almost be a third brother of mine. Goodbye. I won't forget." By this time Crispin was down several branches further, but glancing back up he saw the falcon was gone.

SIX

THE WOLF AGAIN

Climbing down the tree was far easier than climbing up. That helps when you are in a hurry and Crispin dropped down from branch to branch and stopped paying careful attention to what he was doing. And so, as he was turning around on one branch to look for the next, he lost his balance. He fell forward; his heart stopped; his stomach dropped into his sneakers; even the tree stopped breathing, and high above, Malgrin turned sharply in flight to see what would happen.

There was a branch, a narrow branch, and Crispin was just able to grab it with both hands as he fell. He swung wildly in midair, praying that the branch would not break. At least the palms of his hands were so sticky with pitch that there was no problem keeping his grip. He looked down past his chest. There was no branch beneath him that he could see for about fifteen feet, and no branch in front of him, either. Very carefully, by shifting his hands one at a time, he turned himself around. The branch he had fallen off he could just reach with his toes. That did no good; it merely suspended him, more or less horizontally, between the two branches. He would have to get up onto the one he was gripping. So, again, he adjusted one hand to the other side of the branch, walked his feet up the trunk and threw a leg over the branch.

"Dear God, let this hold," seeped out with the perspiration beading his whole body.

With as little extra movement as he could manage, Crispin pulled himself up, and over, until he was straddling the branch facing outwards. Next he had to turn a quarter turn, stand up and try to step back to the original branch. If only there were something else to hold on to besides the big trunk. But there wasn't. He had to pull up his feet and get himself into a squatting position, being very careful that he didn't pitch over backwards. He did it; then slowly he straightened his knees, sliding his shoulder up the rough bark of the tree. He did that, and there he stood, upright, balancing carefully with nothing to steady him except the trunk of the great tree.

The branch Crispin had fallen off was about two feet lower than the one he was standing on, and, mercifully, much thicker. Above and beyond that was another solid branch to hang on to if he dared to make the giant step. He had no choice. He gathered his muscles and stepped out with his right foot, pushing off with his left toes like a diver. His right foot reached the branch and he was already stretching arms and hands to the further branch. He reached it, grasped it, pulled his left foot in . . . and was safe. Only then did he start to tremble, and he realized that he was running with perspiration, into his eyes, down his jaw, down his chest and sides and the small of his back. He closed his eyes as tight as they would go and said, "Oh! Thank you, thank you, thank you."

He did not want to move. For the second time that day he felt that Heaven would mean never having to move again. But the sun kept moving. He was well aware of that. He took a deep breath, opened his eyes, and with more care than ever before, started downward again.

Before long he came to the place where he had left his sweater, his knapsack, and the umbrella. He put his sweater on, laced the umbrella to the outside of the knapsack again, and put that on his back.

The way down got easier as the branches got bigger and closer together, but there were places where Crispin still had to swing around under branches like a monkey and let himself down to the next. Nevertheless, he had learned his lesson and never again lost his concentration or his care.

Finally, and it seemed to take forever, he reached the bottom-most branch, the one as big as or bigger than the path. He strode carefully out to where he had climbed aboard, got down and wrapped both his arms and legs around it and swung himself underneath, let go with his legs and hung straight down at arms length, holding only by the pressure of his hands cupped over opposite sides of the branch. He let go and dropped down, landing at the feet of the great, grey wolf, who stood holding Crispin's high tops.

"I heard you coming and thought you might forget these."

"Thank you. And here's your umbrella." Crispin slipped out of his knapsack, unlaced the umbrella, and handed it to the wolf. "Safe and sound."

"Thank *you*. Was it helpful at all?"

"It gave me a lot of trouble in the beginning but turned out to be a big help later on."

"Like most things," said the wolf. "And thank you for the witch. She wasn't my usual fare—too stringy and tough—but we made do. I had the cover off the pot because the water was seething. She did a jackknife and cut the surface with barely a splash."

By this time Crispin was sitting on the ground, with one sneaker off and was lacing up a hightop with fingers which, because they were blackened with dirt and sticky with pitch, slowed him down. However, having heard the splash all the way up in the tree, he glanced up and saw that the wolf was struggling to keep his face straight. "What was that explosion?" the boy asked.

"Wasn't that a surprise? I chopped up the broomstick and threw the pieces into the fire. The explosion threw me right back on my tail. I was afraid for a minute that I had lost tripod, cauldron, witch, and all, but then that horrific-smelling smoke cleared away and I saw that we were still in business, so to speak. The salt and pepper were practically blown into your hightops, and the spoon curled up like a bed spring. See here." The wolf held out something which, except for the bowl itself, was twisted unrecognizably. Crispin glanced at it briefly but had no time for an examination. He continued lacing.

"You seem to be in a great hurry, young man," remarked the wolf. "Why is that?"

"The sun is practically down"—Crispin stood up and packed his sneakers into the knapsack—"and it's beginning to get dark." He tied up the knapsack and put it on his back with his arms through the loops. "I have to get out of the forest while I can still see the path, and I have quite a ways to go. And I think my family must be very worried about me. I've been away all day so I have to make tracks." He started around the tree, looking for the steps he had come up in the morning.

"But wait a minute," said the wolf, "nothing could be easier. Aren't you forgetting something?"

"No, I think I have everything I came with."

"No, no, no, I mean about going on a journey. Aren't you forgetting the umbrella?"

Crispin stopped. He *had* forgotten the umbrella and what it was good for. "Do you mean I can use it for myself?"

"But of course. Almost anyone can use it who knows how. That's the beauty of the umbrella, and also its problem. Here." The wolf held out the umbrella towards Crispin, who took it, undid the snap and shook out the folds. Then he hesitated.

"But what if I wind up in the wrong place? How could I get back?"

"You won't, not if you're directions are clear. Just keep it simple."

Crispin still hesitated.

"Well," said the wolf, "I can't very well demonstrate since the umbrella has been entrusted to my keeping. But it works just as simply as you made it work for the leopard. Go ahead, the sun is down."

And, indeed, long shadows had gradually crept up the hill and, although there was still a lot of summer dusk left in the air, only the top of the great tree still caught the sunlight. Crispin turned and faced the great tree. He looked up into its branches as high as he could see. He raised the umbrella in salute: "Maybe next time," he breathed. Then he slowly lowered the point to the ground in front of him and turned away.

Gently he opened the umbrella. To the wolf he said, "Thank you. In case I don't see you again. My name is Crispin. And yours?"

"Greyfell."

Crispin could feel his heart beating more and more loudly. He thought this might prove to be more adventure than he had bargained for. He raised the umbrella over his head. Then, very clearly, he said, "Home. Please."

The umbrella remained suspended in midair for a split second and the wolf grabbed it before it fell. "Goodbye," he said. "Until next time."

*

Crispin stood at the bottom of the garden, next to the green bay tree. He wouldn't let himself think about what had just happened, about the roaring of great winds in his ears and the voice of many waters; he hadn't time, anyway.

He raced up the garden paths, his knapsack bumping on his back, past borders and hedges and open geometrical plots, and climbed the steps onto the terrace lawn. There were lights in the house, but only downstairs. Across the lawn he ran and through the garden door into the stone passageway. The kitchen was dark but the door into the dining room was ajar and light shone into the passage. He glanced again at his tell-tale blackened hands and remembered that his mother's tablecloth was white. Nevertheless, he pushed the heavy door open, stepped in, and said, "I'm home."

SEVEN

THE GREEN BAY TREE

"What a liar you are!"

Crispin started up from a sound sleep into wide-wakefulness. It was Tarquin, his older brother. He was sitting, fully clothed, on the end of the bed and was shaking Crispin's foot strenuously beneath the bedclothes. "What a liar!" he repeated.

"Let go of my foot! What are you talking about?" Crispin twisted his leg violently, breaking Tarquin's grip, pulled up both his legs, and sat up. "What lies, what lies?"

They were both talking in harsh whispers, trying not to disturb the rest of the house. The sun was just reaching the horizon and the argument could escalate into a *real* struggle with just a little more pressure or light.

"How could you fill me with such a pack of lies? How could I fall for it?"

"I don't tell lies!" And Crispin launched himself at his brother and the two went crashing to the floor in a mass of flailing knees and elbows and hands. Tarquin was older, taller, heavier, and stronger than Crispin, and more experienced too, and before long he had Crispin down on his back, was sitting on his chest with his knees pressing painfully on Crispin's forearms. "Little liar," taunted Tarquin. Then the door opened.

"What's going on in here?" It was their father.

"Nothing," said Tarquin, rolling off Crispin and standing up.

"It doesn't look like nothing; it doesn't *sound* like nothing. It's a wonder you didn't wake the baby. What's it all about?"

By this time Crispin was also on his feet. "He called me a liar, and I don't tell lies."

"Did you?"

"He is."

"I'm not, I'm not."

"All right, quiet down. Now Tarquin, why did you call your brother a liar?"

"Because he told me a whole cock and bull story about his little trip into the forest: he never even went there, because there isn't any bridge. There's a deep stream all right, but no bridge." And Tarquin looked at his brother with superior contempt.

"Is that why you're dressed so early? You've already been out to the edge of the forest?"

"Yes, Sir."

"You had better go to your room and stay there until your mother calls you for breakfast."

Tarquin went through the connecting door and bathroom into his own room but left the door ajar behind him. His father stepped over and shut it firmly and then turned to his second son. "Well?"

Crispin knew that he was standing on thin ice. Three days ago he had been missing from home for an entire day; that was serious business. He had been missing at breakfast and still missing at lunch, and missing again at dinner. His parents had looked for him, his father staying home from work that day; the farmers from down the way had looked for him, even Tarquin had joined the search, treating it more as a lark than it actually was. There had been an empty milk glass in the sink. His pajamas were hung up in the closet, but his knickers, his shirt and sweater, his high tops and even his sneakers were gone. It was obviously not a kidnapping. Had he run away from home? His bicycle was still in the stone barn across the courtyard, and his father had driven up and down all the nearby roads, but there was no trace, nor had anyone seen a small boy on foot. It had been a long, worrisome, painful day, and when Crispin walked into the dining room after dinner was finished, and announced, "I'm home," his parents had been so relieved that they had not questioned him too closely. His explanation, "I went into the forest," had proved to be sufficient, although his parents had forbidden his going there.

Nevertheless, Crispin had been so full of the adventures of that day that, although understandably reluctant to confide them to his parents, he had, after a day or two of trying to hold everything back, told some of it to his older brother. He had held back about the umbrella and his struggle with the witch but certainly not about climbing the great tree. Tarquin, as the natural trailblazer of the two, had been highly skeptical. He knew that Crispin did a great deal more reading than he and that his younger brother was very imaginative, so he pretty much discounted the whole episode. But Crispin had been so positive and insistent that he finally thought he had better go himself and see. He wasn't one that was willing to be left out of an adventure.

"What's all this about a bridge?" It was his father's question. Crispin explained that at the very end of the woods, right before the forest, there was a deep, swift-flowing stream and that he had discovered a stone bridge that crossed the stream in a single, leaping arch.

"Makes sense to me," said his father: "Woodcutters on the original holding, most likely. Now get dressed immediately and go down and have your breakfast." So Crispin did that.

"And don't start reading anything until after breakfast." And he did that, too.

*

Crispin put his dishes from breakfast on the drain board of the kitchen sink and hurried outside. His father had left for work, his mother was upstairs busy with the baby, Justin. Henriette (the cook) had her hands in soapy hot water in the sink, and Tarquin had disappeared. He was probably on his bicycle going over to play with the farmer's boys. He would probably tell them everything that Crispin had told him and Crispin's cheeks burned.

Of course there was a bridge. He had crossed it himself. How could anybody that was looking for it not find it? Once again he hurried across the terrace lawn and down the steps into the garden, down through the garden past hedges and pools, and finally out the gate into the orchard. Through the orchard he went, under the gate into the meadow, across the meadow and again under the fence into the woods. The last time he had been going in as straight a line as possible until he got into the woods, and then he followed old cart tracks and animal trails, but still trying to keep as straight as possible. He did the same this morning. Deeper and deeper into the darkening woods he walked. The trail he was following skirted a large tree and Crispin silently stepped out of the trail and put his back against the tree. He was being followed. How did he know that? Because, out of habit, he was trying to move as silently as possible and his step, therefore, was irregular from time to time. But the step behind him was absolutely regular and determined. On glancing back he could see nothing, but he *knew*. He waited behind the tree. It was Tarquin.

"Bang: You're dead."

"Oh, nice going: How did you know I was following you?"

"We scouts don't tell our secrets."

"Never mind: just show me this bridge."

They moved on, Indian file, and had not gone but about fifty yards further when, quite suddenly; they came out onto the banks of the stream.

There was no bridge.

Crispin turned pale. The stream was the same, the forest on the other side looked right. This *should* be the place. He was crestfallen and felt betrayed. In fact, he looked so bad that Tarquin patted him on the shoulder. "Never mind," he said, "it was a good story anyway. C'mon, let's go home."

"It wasn't a story," cried Crispin, his heart almost breaking. "Go on. I'll be along."

And he *did* follow, eventually, after examining the bank of the stream for at least fifty yards in both directions. Not a trace of a bridge or any foundations for one. Nothing. But he hadn't dreamt it. He was sure of that.

And so a very perplexed young boy, digging a tear of frustration from the corner of each eye, followed his older brother home.

*

That night there was company for dinner. Crispin washed his face and hands as he always had to before dinner. Then he put on a shirt and tie as he knew was expected. He stood in his window looking out and seeing nothing, waiting to be called. He felt numb and completely alone, although he did not say this to himself or even recognize it. When he was called, both he and Tarquin went downstairs to the library, not down the circular stone steps in the tower, by far the oldest part of the house, but down the broad, oaken, "new stairs," with their intricately carved balustrades.

Tarquin and Crispin were introduced to the two guests, a business associate and his wife. They said, "How do you do, sir," and "ma'am," "Yes, ma'am," and "No, sir," as occasion indicated, and went in to dinner. There were candles on the table. Crispin liked that and felt comforted by the semi-darkness. Furthermore, when there were guests, the rule was that "little boys should be seen and not heard," so Crispin felt free to brood his own thoughts. He tried to smile or laugh when everyone else laughed, and look as though he were paying attention. But once he missed a direct question and had to be prompted by his mother. Otherwise he acquitted himself well enough. He kept his back straight and his elbows off the table; he didn't slurp his soup or try to pack too much onto his fork. Then there was a pause in the dinner.

The dishes were cleared away. Henriette was bringing in the dessert. Crispin knew that he could not ask to be excused until after dessert and he wouldn't miss *that* anyway. Conversation paused as the adults reflected on the dinner or twisted the stems of their wine glasses. Without warning, into this momentary silence, Crispin, in a clear, distinct voice, declared, "The green bay tree!"

That must be it! He had been over and over the matter again and again until his mind was drawing blanks and had turned off, as it were. Then it had occurred to him, in that empty-minded void, the one thing that was different, that he had done on his first expedition to the forest but not on his second.

Could that really be it? Something so simple? He had pulled a leaf off the green bay tree just before he went out through the gate into the orchard, and had dropped the leaf into the stream as he went across the bridge.

"Crispin, are you getting sleepy?" his father at the head of the table asked. "Did you want to be excused without dessert?"

"I'm very fond of bay leaves, myself; couldn't cook without them; how lovely that you have a whole tree." The woman sitting across from him smiled. Tarquin was looking at him curiously from the other side of the table, and the man next to Crispin said, "I hear you're a great climber of trees, young man: used to climb them myself at your age. But I wouldn't have thought a green bay tree offered much of a challenge." He chuckled to himself.

Everyone had turned to look and, even in the candlelight, Crispin blushed very red. He could feel the heat all the way up to the roots of his hair. He glanced at his mother but she turned away and busied herself with the coffee cups. When he dared, he glanced at his father but he seemed preoccupied. Fortunately, at that moment, Henriette set in front of him a plate of chocolate steamed pudding covered with ice cream sauce, so he seized his fork, muttered, "Yessir, you're right, sir," and dug in.

*

Crispin, in his pajama pants, had brushed his teeth, washed his face, again, and, turning out the light in the bathroom, went into his own room and shut the door. He put on his pajama top and went over to the window, knelt down on the window seat and leaned out. The night sky was agleam with stars and he said his prayers there, thinking more about the beauty of the stars than what he was actually saying. Then, once again, he recalled his realization from the dinner table: how, on his first journey to the forest, he had pulled a leaf from the green bay tree, carried it with him all the way to the stream, and dropped it in as he crossed over the bridge. It struck him that on his way back, when he had held the green umbrella open over his head and had said, "Home. Please," he had emerged just at that very spot, next to the green bay tree. Yes, that must be the secret of the bridge, and he would put it to the test as soon as possible. Tomorrow; then maybe Tarquin would learn a thing or two; if he bothered to tell him at all.

The connecting door to Tarquin's room opened and his brother walked in. "Are you all right?" he asked.

"Yes. I'm OK."

"What was that about a green bay tree: at dinner?"

"Nothing."

"Sure?"

Silence.

"Well, go to bed."

"Go to bed yourself."

Before his father or mother came up to look in on him, he stood up on the window seat (which his imagination immediately turned into a dock), stepped across onto his bed (a boat), settled himself down under the covers, the boat pulled away from the shore and before very long the boy was fast asleep, "rocked in the cradle of the deep."

EIGHT

TEMPESTS

Crispin was finishing his breakfast at the kitchen table. In fact, he was down to his last piece of toast and marmalade—he had saved the piece with the most butter and marmalade on it for the end. Once again he was the last one to eat because, as was quite usual, he had been distracted by a book while he was getting dressed. Crispin was one of those children who could get through three chapters with one sock on and one off. Now his mother came into the kitchen and, seeing that he was finished, took his dishes and put them into the sink.

"Don't lick your fingers." Crispin had already begun.

"But there's butter and marmalade on them."

"Don't lick your fingers, it's not polite. Be more careful when you eat."

Crispin sighed, "Yes, ma'am," and wiped his sticky fingers on his napkin. What a waste it seemed.

"And don't forget, you're going to mind your baby brother for me this morning." He had forgotten. He was just about to launch himself down through the garden and rediscover the bridge at the end of the woods, *after* brushing his teeth, and now his morning had just been canceled. There was no way out. He remembered promising, and promises must be kept. He knew if he tried arguing he would be told not to whine. So, like most boys who are really good at heart, he went upstairs and brushed his teeth, got his book from his room and came back down. He paused just briefly on the landing of the tower stairs and looked across the valleys and forest to his great tree. He could see clearly the point at which he had stopped climbing on that memorable day. *Soon again,* he thought, and continued downstairs.

"I'll be out on the lawn," he told his mother, and went out quickly through the garden door . . . lest his mother ask him to dry the breakfast dishes.

The morning was still fresh, its freshness lying on the grass and under the trees, but not as fresh as it had been earlier. Soon his mother came out carrying Justin and a large quilt with blue and red star-bursts on it. The quilt she spread out in the sunshine where it would gradually be covered by shade as the day grew warmer, and set the baby in the middle of it.

Actually, Crispin liked playing with his baby brother from time to time. Justin was getting steadier on his legs every day and it was a job to keep him mostly on the quilt. So they rolled and tumbled and laughed and Crispin made up all sorts of impromptu games. These consisted mostly of Crispin imitating Justin and Justin trying to imitate Crispin, who turned himself into roosters and cows and sheep, dogs and cats and then into other babies, much to the delight of his brother. Then, when baby Justin began to grow tired, Crispin told him the entire story of his first expedition into the forest to climb his great tree. He told him about the wolf and the witch, how the witch had tumbled into the wolf's pot, how Greyfell, (the wolf) had broken up the witch's broomstick and tossed it onto his fire, and the terrific explosion it had made. The he told Justin about the leopard and the falcon and even about the enchanted umbrella, things that he had not even attempted to tell Tarquin. Gradually the baby fell asleep. Crispin modulated his voice to a gentle crooning drone and then stopped altogether. The baby was sitting in the circle made by Crispin's crossed legs, leaning against him and becoming heavier and heavier every minute that his brother had to sit still and not move.

We chew, we chew; cack cack cack.

Crispin looked up.

We chew.

It was the peregrine. Crispin extricated himself from the baby as quickly and gently as he could and stood up. Circling above the maple tree, the falcon was crying out with great urgency, *We chew.*

"Malgrin, Malgrin! Here, here I am! Come bird!"

And Crispin instinctively held up his fist. The falcon swooped down and, braking with wing-feathers and tail, came to a rest on the outstretched fist, his talons lightly but firmly holding the boy's knuckles. Then he let out a cascade of guttural, nasal rasps and whirring ratchets like a cadenza.

"Oh Malgrin! I can't understand you anymore. What's the trouble? Why can't I understand you? Tell me, tell me: what's the matter?" Abruptly the falcon pushed off from his uneasy perch, circled once above the boy's head and darted off across the meadow and woods towards the forest.

Crispin stood there completely bewildered. The pounding in his heart and the knot in the pit of his stomach told him that something was seriously wrong. Perhaps his great tree was threatened or something even worse, if there could *be* anything worse. He felt that he was needed desperately and that he had been summoned, that Malgrin had been sent to fetch him; but by whom? And for what? He also remembered his conversation with this falcon high up in the great tree and now he could not understand him at all. Why was that?

He turned back towards the baby asleep on the quilt and discovered that his mother was standing in the shadow of one of the terrace trees. She was watching him silently but with intense curiosity. She stood there looking at him, holding his gaze with her own, then she walked slowly forward to the other side of the quilt. Little Justin lay sleeping between them.

"What bird was that?"

"A falcon, a peregrine falcon I think they call it. There's a colored plate of it in Father's big book." He knew that that was not the answer to his mother's question but he hoped that it would be taken as acceptable.

"No, no. You called it a name. What bird was that?"

"Malgrin."

"Malgrin: How did you know that's its name?"

His mother's gaze still held his own. He felt that she could read every thought that crossed his mind. Moreover, he had never lied to his parents in all of his short life and he hoped that he never would. But right now he longed for some other answer than the one he knew he must give.

"He told me."

"You asked it?"

"Yes."

"And it told you its name was Malgrin?"

"Yes. That's his name."

"You have been reading too many books, young man. Do you have a fever? Come here and let me feel your forehead."

Crispin walked slowly around the end of the quilt and stood by his mother. He felt relieved that he no longer had to look into her eyes. She put a cool hand on his brow and said, "No, no fever. Have you been sleeping all right?"

"Yes, fine."

"Well, after you have your lunch, perhaps you had better lie down for a while, *without* reading, and give your poor brain a rest."

"But, I . . ."

"No "*but*s." I'm taking Justin inside. You will please fold up the quilt and bring it along. I think we're going to have some weather." She gathered up the baby so gently that he didn't wake up, and turned and went indoors.

Only then did the spring release for Crispin and he again became aware of what was going on around him. The wind had already folded over a large portion of the parti-colored quilt, and the sunshine had faded; there were no shadows anywhere. He folded the quilt over once, twice, as neatly as the increasing wind would permit. Then again, kneeling down, he tried to smooth it out. He stood up, picked up the quilt, and looked up. What could he possibly do? Day growing darker and darker: wind beginning to thresh the trees and tug at the quilt, the air smelling heavily of rain, and that terrible note of urgency in the falcon's voice threading its way through his memory. A crack of thunder split the air nearby and he could hear his mother beginning to close windows.

"Crispin, hurry inside!" He made a dash for the open French windows and turned for one final look. He could see no bird soaring against the black, hurrying clouds. Then the rain fell.

The storm raged much of the afternoon, blowing rain in great sheets against the house, and plastering leaves to the walls and windows. The wind blew the rain so hard against the western windows that water began to seep in around the edges. Crispin and his mother went from window to window, putting towels on the windowsills to soak up the water before it stained wallpapers or floors. Lights flickered and came on again. The big blue wooden gate from the road into the courtyard worked loose and started to thrash back and forth. He saw this from his window and darted out to secure it. He was drenched to the skin in a moment and just missed getting knocked down by the heavy gate as it swung. His mother shouted, "Good work, Crispin!" from the sheltered doorway. She had him take off his soaking clothes in the kitchen where the water made no difference on the massive slate tiles. Before he was finished, his mother was back with a big warm towel and his bathrobe and slippers. So he rubbed himself down vigorously, as directed, and then ran upstairs to put on dry clothes and roll himself up in a blanket. Curtains of driven rain obscured the meadows and fields across the road so he sat in the window seat, watching rivers and lakes form and reform amongst the cobbles of the yard.

Then it was over. The storm, like a great, wrathful buffalo snorting thunder and lightning, hurried off elsewhere to the east. The sky, scrubbed clean of every shred, deepened to a most transparent blue. A bird chirped and hushed, and the stillness was as noticeable as the storm.

Tarquin bicycled in from the farmers' where he had ridden out the storm in the hay barn and he and Crispin were set to picking up the branches and twigs that had been ripped down from the terrace trees.

*

Later that afternoon Crispin was sitting in the sleepy-hollow chair in the library. Once a very ample farm office, it had been converted into an adequate library when it was no longer needed as an office. It had a fireplace, with blackened andirons and a very old hearth broom, a stone floor partially covered by a heavy rug, and books on shelves that rose from floor to ceiling. For Crispin it was a hideaway and sanctuary. Having been told not to read, he sat deep in the chair with the bird book in his lap. He had opened it to the colored plate of the peregrine falcon. Yes, that was the one all right, right down to the rakish black mask and sideburns. He gazed and gazed at the colored plate but his thoughts were far away, rising in easy circles above the great pine tree where he had first met Malgrin. How he wished he could just fly out there, learn what the trouble was, and be back in time for dinner. Then he wouldn't be missed from home and he would not have to make any excuses or, worse, explanations. He had pulled both legs up into the chair and sat cross-legged like an Indian brave. Anyone passing the open library door and glancing in would have no idea he was there.

Perhaps he had dozed off or just fallen into a deep trance, because he didn't hear his father drive into the courtyard nor his mother come down the stairs. He gradually became conscious of a blur of voices but was startled alert and wary when he heard his mother say, "He knows."

"Who does?"

"Crispin."

"Yes, he would be the most likely. How much does he know?"

"He certainly knows the bird and its name. I found him trying to talk to it this morning just before the storm. But of course he couldn't. Not here, at any rate; and about the bay tree and the bridge. But we suspected that."

"Anything else?"

"I don't know. He has been very close-mouthed about the whole thing. He said the bird told him its name when he asked it. What are we going to do?"

The answer, if there was one, Crispin was unable to hear since his parents had passed out of earshot up the stairs. He climbed quickly out of the chair, put the book away on the bottom shelf where he had found it, and sloped off down the stone passageway and up the tower stairs to his own room. What could this possibly mean? What did his parents know about the forest? As much as, or more, than he did, apparently. But why were they so concerned about *his* knowing? These were the sorts of questions making a racket in his mind.

We chew, we chew!

He could still hear the urgent note in Malgrin's voice. That cry was like another station on a radio that can't quite be tuned out. Then he remembered his mother's question, "How did you know that's its name?" As though *she* had known all along. He longed to turn to someone for help and advice but there didn't seem to be anyone at all. Not Tarquin. He was completely unconvinced by Crispin's story. He would scoff at the whole thing and tell him to grow up. And then go and tell their parents, maybe, or blurt everything out at table.

And his father and mother? The boy felt that something nameless and dark had come to stand between his parents and himself. It is a terrible trial for a young boy to begin to distrust his parents. He wanted to go to them and ask what they knew about the forest and the creatures in it. But his heart told him that if they denied knowing anything, he would be lost. He had never really had any secrets from them before, but somehow he had felt that he couldn't, or *shouldn't*, tell them about the wolf and the witch, the leopard and the falcon. Now he had discovered that they knew even more than he did, and seemed very concerned that he had learned anything at all. They would forbid him, absolutely, to go there. Then what would he do? He turned on every light in his darkening room. But it did not help.

"*We chew, we chew.*"

"Crispin, dinner's on the table. Come down at once."

He would return to the forest tomorrow. Early: before anyone else was up!

NINE

TRYCE

Of course the bridge was there, as Crispin knew it would be. Somehow, as he pulled a leaf from the green bay tree, all shadows of doubts had vanished. Even as he approached along the final trail in the woods, no *IF* had floated through his mind. But he did examine the bridge carefully—absolutely solid stone—and at the top of the arch he jumped up and down with both feet—no imaginary bridge, this—before dropping the leaf over the parapet and hurrying down the other side.

The path awaited him and up he went through the taller trees beginning to fill with light. The path rose steadily, but not steeply, and on this morning Crispin carried nothing with him.

He had left his knapsack and canteen at home since he hoped to be back, if not for breakfast, for lunch. He was not into summer shorts but still in his knickers and he had his hightops on because of yesterday's drenching storm. Since he was not planning to climb into the great tree at all, he had left his sneakers behind as well. Nor had he stopped long enough to eat anything for breakfast. He loped downhill and across the stepping stones laid out so carefully in the noisy stream. Here he did pause long enough to drink a cupped handful of water.

He sprang up the first set of steps. He continued walking and climbing while at the back of his mind the question stuck like a burr he could not reach: Why had the falcon sounded so urgent, even desperate? He could not make it out but hurried anxiously toward the great tree and the wolf beneath it. Although moving rapidly, the hike seemed to take him even longer than the first time. But sooner or later all journeys come to an end.

Crispin raced up the first few of the last broad flight of steps crying out, "Greyfell, Greyfell!" and then stopped stone-still in his tracks as he glanced up at the great pine tree. It looked ancient and fragile. Its trunk and branches, which had been almost black with glints of red and brown in them, were now all silvery against the green of the other trees, and its layers and clusters of needles looked pale. He knew that the tree must be very old indeed because it was so huge around and so enormously tall. Before, it had seemed fresh and almost young, but now it had begun to look all of its many, many years. This change had taken place just over the last few days.

"My tree! What's happening to my tree?"

Crispin started up the rest of the steps and then caught sight of Greyfell, the great grey wolf, sitting on his haunches at the base of the great tree. He stopped again. Something was different about Greyfell as well. He too looked older, more dignified; there was something almost regal about him, but haggard, too, as though from burdens too heavy to bear.

"Your tree is dying, Crispin, and I can't save it. But perhaps you can. You have come just in time. We were afraid that you might not come at all, especially when Malgrin couldn't make you understand."

"Yes, yes . . . but the tree?"

"It will be dead in two days unless you can save it."

"But why? And *how?*"

"That's *two* questions: which one first?"

"How?"

"There were two broomsticks made out of the wood of this tree, or, at least, a tree growing on this very spot. One was put to evil uses—that's the one you know—and was destroyed by me. I think I made a mistake throwing that broomstick into the fire. You remember the explosion it made?"

Malgrin, perched on a branch in the tree just above their heads, interrupted, "That's why I came to find you in such a hurry. And when you couldn't understand me I didn't know what to do or how to start doing it. And then your mother came out of the house so I took off—in two senses."

Greyfell continued, "The other broom has only been put to good uses, so far as anyone can tell. Now, that broomstick, when thrust into a knothole in this tree, will immediately become living wood again and begin to grow. And the same will happen to the tree."

"And that will fix everything?"

"Yes. Or at least it will restore the tree. But it must be accomplished within seven days from the destruction of the broom. We have already lost five."

"But where *is* this other broom? How can we find it? And who says only seven days, anyway?"

"Like all youngsters, you ask questions in bunches. It was my grandfather who told me "seven days" when he made me Custodian of the Forest. About the broom, nobody knows where it is."

"You mean nobody at all?"

"Nobody that I know: You see, the broomstick disappeared some centuries ago, just at the beginning of—"

At this point the peregrine falcon, on his branch overhead, sneezed loudly and made the wolf cock his head and look up. Now, since falcons rarely, if ever, sneeze, this one was probably an attempt to interrupt Greyfell. But it was unnecessary—Crispin did it far more effectively.

"But if nobody knows where it is, how on earth can we find it? And *where?*" For the first time in his young life, Crispin faced a situation that seemed completely hopeless.

"For generations my family has been through every inch of this forest, and even beyond, and never have we found a trace of it. Malgrin and *his* family have combed the air . . . Excuse me, I did not intend to be funny in this serious situation. Surveyed from above, as far as falcons can fly, and . . . ." Greyfell looked up to Malgrin.

"No. Nothing: we saw everything, found . . . nothing."

Greyfell continued, "The moles and groundhogs, although understandably reluctant to talk to us, have been canvassed as well. They found nothing in the earth. Likewise the stippled trout have investigated every brook, stream, and river right down to the salt; there the salmon took over. Nothing: We thought, since the broom was made of wood, we could forget about fire. Nevertheless, even the salamanders—"

"The salamanders?"

"Yes. You see, the ancients believed that salamanders lived in fire because of their iridescent skin; nevertheless, when we asked them, the salamanders were no help."

"Stop! This just gets worse and worse, Greyfell. How can we be in a hurry if we have no place to look?" Crispin was fighting back mounting impatience and grief.

"In a hurry: yes, just two days counting this one. But I do think we have a place to begin. Follow me."

The grey wolf went off around the vast trunk of the tree to where his cauldron hung on its tripod. There was no fire burning under it now and Greyfell removed some of the blackened stones and began digging in the ashes. Grey ash dust rose in puffs and scarves.

"Just hand me my spoon, if you would be so kind."

"I should have brought you a new spoon," said Crispin, handing the wolf the twisted iron spoon that had been damaged in the explosion.

"No real need as yet. Just hold the pot out of the way while I pry up this brick." Crispin saw that there was a layer of bricks underneath the ashes. One of these Greyfell pried up with the handle of the spoon so that he could lift it out. Beneath the brick was a deep container into which Greyfell reached and extracted what appeared to be some sort of scroll. That is exactly what it was.

"There," he said, handing the scroll to Crispin, "not damaged by the heat, I hope, nor by the damp. When I was made Custodian I built my fire over the bricks to conceal them, and the secret has never been discovered."

"So far as you know," the falcon added from above, where he was watching expectantly from his perch.

"True. But there are so rarely interlopers, although I suspect that witch was hunting for more than the umbrella."

The scroll had been carefully wrapped in a waxy sort of cloth to keep the damp out, and this had been sealed with a large seal. Crispin looked closely at the seal, and Malgrin and Greyfell looked at one another. An insignia had been pressed deep into the red wax seal. "It's a leopard," Crispin said softly to himself, and with a deft movement of his thumb, he broke the seal and unrolled the scroll.

The parchment had been closely written over in a hand both crabbed and dark, and Crispin had to turn it this way and that before he was sure which end was the top. He scowled. He squinted. Gradually (because he liked puzzles) the writing clarified. He read it aloud, pausing only in places where the ink had betrayed the pen and penman. This is what it said:

From the destruction of the broom, seven days,
But only seven years will win it.
Whether in water, earth, air, or fire,
Whether in all or none of these,
That the second broom ye shall discover,
I doubt.

Failing that:
Try across the Wider Water.
Longshanks, he the hamper has.
Try to find the Black Witch Blood;
From that a new direction take,
Learning as ye go along
To have done . . .
With my forest.

At the very bottom, in very definite, capital letters (as though the author was making a special effort) was the one word: **TRYCE.**

"It's not very nice," said Crispin. He could almost feel malevolence breathing from the parchment.

"Wicked, that's what it is," said Greyfell. And Malgrin ruffled his feathers and drew his head deep between his shoulders.

"And it doesn't seem to be any help at all," Crispin continued. "How can you do in seven days what takes seven years? And anyway, we only have two left!" He threw down the scroll angrily and got up and began to pace about. Somewhere something was at work to frustrate his good intentions and destroy his tree, and it made him angry.

"Anger solves nothing." Greyfell had remained absolutely motionless, his eyes narrowed to slits, the yellow fires burning within. "And as to that," he said, "how old, exactly, are you?"

"Seven: going on eight."

"Seven: the perfect number. Well, maybe the scroll means that only someone seven years old will win it."

"Oh, Greyfell! Do you think that can be it? Could it really mean that?"

"It is a legitimate interpretation," said the wolf, and the slits of his eyes narrowed even further. "Malgrin?"

"Legitimate."

"Well young man, it appears you have a journey to make." Greyfell took charge. "Have you had any breakfast yet?"

"No."

"Too bad, you'll need it. And you don't have your knapsack with you. We must send you home for breakfast, your knapsack, some more clothes, and provisions for the rest of the day. How long will that take you?"

"It wouldn't take as long if I could use the umbrella."

"Nothing could be easier." Greyfell led the way among the vast roots of the tree and handed Crispin the green umbrella.

Crispin had begun to be very conscious of time slipping away, so he said, "It's too bad there isn't some way of taking it with me; then I could use it in both directions and save more time."

"But of course there is. It works quite simply. Instead of opening it up completely, giving your destination, and leaving the umbrella behind, you begin to close it slowly, at the same time giving your destination. Then it goes with you. And while you're gone, since time is of the essence, Malgrin and I will make . . . arrangements."

TEN

CLOCKS, WATCHES, TEMPERS

Crispin held the umbrella over his head and began to collapse it slowly. As he did so he said, "Home, please," and finished folding up the umbrella beside the green bay tree at the bottom of the garden. He hung up the umbrella carefully in the tree where it was out of sight—"Who would pass this way, anyway?"—and started up the walk. He stopped and went back. Should he take it with him? Or would it be safer here? It would certainly be undiscovered in the tree, but . . . he reached up and . . . took it with him up the garden walks.

*

"Good morning, Yettie, have I missed breakfast?"

Henriette looked around from the stove. "No, Crispin, you haven't missed breakfast, but your mother's been looking for you." Crispin glanced at the cottage clock on the shelf over the stove: 7:30.

"Are they still at table?" He was hoping he might *just* get away without having to meet his mother or father. No such luck.

"Just getting started, really: what would you like?"

By this time Crispin had closed the kitchen door into the hall and leaned the umbrella against the wall behind it. "What is there?"

"The usual: oatmeal for growing boys, toast, bacon and eggs if you'd like; as I suppose you would since you've been out already, although doing what at this early hour I can't imagine. At least your high tops aren't muddy on my kitchen floor," glancing down at his feet.

He had scraped carefully and used the mat before he came in; he thought of the journey ahead of him and said, "I'll have it all, please. And brown sugar on the oatmeal."

"I don't forget. Now wash your hands if you've been out and I'll be right in with your orange juice and oatmeal. The brown sugar's on the table."

He went into the pantry and washed his hands and passed on into the dining room.

"Here's Crispin now; good morning," said his father from the other end of the table.

"Good morning, Dad. Good morning, Mother." He slid into his chair and unfolded his napkin over his lap. Tarquin looked up quizzically from his plate.

"You're up early. Or are you just getting in?" Tarquin was used to his mother having to call Crispin for breakfast two or three times before he actually appeared. Frequently enough he was still in his bathrobe and pajamas and had to be sent back again to get dressed, depending on how late it was.

Yettie put Crispin's orange juice and oatmeal down in front of him and moved the brown sugar within reach.

"Thank you, Henriette." His mother didn't like the boys to call Henriette 'Yettie.'

"Grace," his mother said as he picked up his spoon. Crispin said it. Then he looked up at Tarquin and said, "I'm just getting in."

"Were you out on a bat, or what?"

"Don't be clever, Tarquin." That was his father. Crispin put two spoons full of brown sugar and some milk on his oatmeal and began to spoon it down his throat. He glanced at the clock on the mantel. It was going on 7:45.

"Don't eat so fast, Crispin. Are you in a hurry?"

"No, ma'am."

"Did you go into the forest again?" his father asked. It was a completely innocent sounding question and asked in precisely that tone of voice, but it had begun to have a history attached to it. And Tarquin sat back in his chair and waited expectantly.

How did he figure that? Crispin asked himself. *I could have gone anywhere and done anything, on foot or on my bicycle.* He felt as though a finger had been pressed down on a bruise.

"Yes, sir."

His brother smirked skeptically and went back to his breakfast. There could be trouble there, but it was a bridge he couldn't cross now.

"You know we told you not to go into the forest. This is the second time you've disobeyed your mother and me."

"But Dad, it's perfectly safe!"

"You could easily get lost."

"No, there's paths and . . ." He stopped before he said too much. The last thing he wanted to do was antagonize his father and mother, and yet they seemed to know all about it. He must remember to ask Greyfell about that. And the clock was moving on towards 8:00.

"Let's say no more about it at the table," suggested his mother.

Henriette deftly removed his empty cereal bowl and in its place set down a plate of bacon and eggs, three pieces of freshly buttered toast, and a cup full of hot cocoa. The cocoa had a marshmallow floating in it.

"Thank you, Yet— . . . Henriette." He could tell he had an ally there. Fortunately, Tarquin did not notice the marshmallow. He would have howled had he seen because he hadn't one in his cocoa.

Breakfast went on that way interminably, it seemed, and the boy tried to keep from glancing too frequently at the clock. But then Tarquin was excused and his father left for the office and Crispin finished his toast, being careful *not* to lick his fingers. His mother was having more coffee, but she excused him and he took his dishes with him into the pantry, left them on the drain board of the sink, and went into the kitchen.

"Yettie, would you please pack up some provisions for me? Sandwiches for lunch . . . and dinner too?"

"Are you taking a trip, Crispin?"

"It's a journey, a quest, probably, not a trip, and I have to get started as soon as possible."

Henriette was used to the imaginative ways of the young boy and always tried to humor him by asking leading question, although his mother was not sure that was the right thing to do. Now she asked, "How long will you be gone?"

Crispin had gone to the door to retrieve the umbrella. "I only have two days, counting this one," he said.

"Two days for what?" It was his mother's voice and, as Crispin turned to see her standing in the pantry door, he tried to keep the umbrella concealed behind him. He could think of nothing to say so he just stood there, his mind unreeling through all sorts of possibilities, none of them satisfactory.

"I asked you a question. Two days for what?"

"To find a broom." Something had to be said and that at least was the truth.

"There's one in the broom closet. Henriette will be happy to let you use it. What are you holding behind your back?"

Crispin could feel a blush spring immediately to his cheeks and tiny beads of perspiration at his hairline and goose bumps across his scalp. He wished mightily that he had left the umbrella hanging in the green bay tree. "It's an umbrella," he said.

"May I see it?" Crispin handed the umbrella to his mother. In doing so he felt as though it had traveled an enormous distance and was forever beyond his grasp. He was afraid he had lost his time, his tree, everything.

"It's not one of ours, is it? Where did you get it?"

He wanted to run, he wanted to hide, he wished he were dead, he wanted to tell his mother everything and nothing at all. He was very aware of Henriette going about her business and making his sandwiches, but listening intently as well, and the cottage clock seemed to be ticking noisily inside his very heart.

"I borrowed it."

"It's a very good one; you must be sure to return it." And she handed the umbrella back to him. "Now ask Henriette if you can borrow her broom, and perhaps you had better sweep out your room with it . . . and stay there until I tell you." She went out into the hall, closing the kitchen door behind her and Crispin sagged noticeably with relief.

"Well, that was a close one, wasn't it?"

"Oh, Yettie, I'm still swallowing my stomach."

"There's more to this than meets the eye," she said shrewdly, "and don't think your mother doesn't know it."

"I know, I know. Do you think she'll lock me in?"

"No. Not since she's told you to stay there. Shall I bring your provisions up when I finish?"

"Yes please."

"I'll put in a piece of the apple pie. You'll have to manage as best you can without a fork."

"Thank you, Yettie, and thank you for the marshmallow."

"Say no more about it." Crispin turned to go. "Don't you want to take the broom up with you?" Her eyes twinkled behind her spectacles.

"I suppose I ought."

"Or you could use the one in the upstairs closet; that might be better for your room."

"Right." he went. He ran up the tower stairs (he was still too short to take them two at a time) and into his room. He had been gone for more than an hour, a wasted hour, an hour he might need before his quest was done. He put the umbrella on his bed, got out his knapsack and tried to think what he ought to put in it: his sneakers for sure, another pair of socks in case, underwear, another shirt and his blue sweater . . . . a comb and his toothbrush, but no paste lest it go squish in his knapsack.

"Well, well, if it isn't the Forest Wanderer," said Tarquin walking into Crispin's room from his own. "How did you get across the stream this time?"

"Elementary, my dear Watson," said Crispin. "You didn't knock."

"I never do. What new adventure are you going to dazzle me with this time?" Crispin's heart sank. He felt he would rather deal with his mother than with his older brother.

Meanwhile, Tarquin had picked up the umbrella, curled his left arm over his head, said, "On guard!" and started lunging at Crispin.

"I'm unarmed. Leave off. And put that down."

"You're no fun. I see you're packing up. Running away from home?"

"No. And don't open the umbrella inside; it's bad luck."

"Old wives' tale:" the umbrella went up and Tarquin started rotating it rapidly over his head. Like lightning out of a clear sky, a thought flashed through Crispin's brain. He put it aside but it persisted. Then the sight of Tarquin with the umbrella proved to be too much.

"Isn't there someplace you'd rather be?"

"Nope. I like it right here, annoying you." Crispin felt his anger rising rapidly as Tarquin continued to horse around with the umbrella. He knew that if he got into a physical struggle with Tarquin he would almost certainly lose and the umbrella might get damaged beyond repair.

A tap came at the door. It was Yettie with the provisions. "Tarquin, your mother's looking for you. She wants you to get your bicycle and go to the store."

"Oh rats! Well, it's better than hanging around here with someone 'confined to quarters.'" He collapsed the umbrella, rolled it up, put it under his arm, and started for the door.

"Leave my umbrella!" Crispin bellowed hoarsely. He was just about to spring onto Tarquin's back when Yettie opened the door, extracted the umbrella from under Tarquin's arm as he went past, and pushed him firmly out the door, placing her ample frame in the doorway.

"Tarquin, I want you to go into the village for me. Get your bicycle." His mother stood at the other end of the hall holding baby Justin in her arms. Yettie shut Crispin's door quietly from inside. There was a whispered consultation about the provisions; Yettie cautioned Crispin not to go so far that he couldn't get home for dinner; then she left.

Crispin packed the provisions into his knapsack and tied the lacings. He looked at the watch on his desk. He gasped. It was 9:30 already! He closed the watch and stuffed both watch, chain, and its little gold penknife into his pocket. The watch had been his grandfather's. His parents had given it to Crispin to keep on his desk so that he could keep better track of time until he was old enough for a wrist watch. However, that scheme had not produced the desired effect. Now, for better or for worse, Crispin had begun to live a life measured by clocks and watches.

He picked up his knapsack and set it behind the door, with the umbrella leaning against it; then he opened the door until it was pushing against the knapsack. His mother, glancing in, would be unable to see either knapsack or umbrella, unless, of course, she was coming from the *other* direction, and looked through the crack made by the open door. Under those circumstances, both knapsack and umbrella were quite visible, so he closed the door again about halfway. It still didn't work. He put the articles in his closet, closed *that* door, and reopened his bedroom door until it touched the wall behind it. Now, if his mother passed, she would be reminded that he was confined, and would, he hoped, relent.

He went to his desk, sat down, opened a book, and gazed out the window. He could not read. He looked at the big watch—9:45. Once again feeling that the world had set its hand against him, he took his book off the desk and went to the window seat beyond the bed. Here he could keep a lookout for Tarquin's return.

He had already disobeyed his parents twice. Now, if he left his room without permission, that would make *three* times. And he was going to the forest again—four. On the other hand, he was not going to leave his room in any ordinary way—down stairs and out through doors—that might put the number back to three, but he knew he was wrong there. The fat was sure to be in the fire anyway, because he would not only miss dinner, he would not be home at all for a night and almost two days, and all that without permission. Then again, if his mother waited too long, Tarquin would be back from the store. That could cause a whole new set of difficulties.

He went to the open door and listened. He could hear no sounds down the hall from either the nursery or his parents' bedroom. He went to the window, leaned out, and looked up the road. Bad luck! Tarquin was just topping the rise and would be back in minutes.

"Don't lean out the window, Crispin, you might fall." His mother stood in the doorway. She had spoken very definitely, but gently, so as not to startle him.

"Yes, ma'am." A concession: "May I please leave my room now?"

"On one condition: that you promise not to go back to the forest again. *Ever.* Promise me that and you are free to go out."

"I can't promise that."

"What do you mean, you can't promise that? You are only seven years old. I've never heard such a thing!"

"Mother, I have to go back. I do, I do. I'll be all right. You'll see. Really, I will. You've got to let me go."

"The forest is a dangerous place. I know. How many times do I have to tell you? I won't have you going there."

Both of their voices had risen, although neither was shouting. Crispin's eyes filled with tears of frustration and woe, and his mother looked very pale, with glints in her eyes. She said, "Now, promise me, *immediately,* that you won't go!"

"I can't. I won't."

"All right, then," and she turned and, taking the key, closed and locked the door from the outside.

"Mother, I'm home from the store! Where's Crispin?" That was Tarquin from the bottom of the tower stairs.

"He's locked in his room."

"Holy cow! What's been going on?" It was Tarquin, at the top of the stairs, outside the door.

"Never you mind: just go someplace and behave yourself."

Crispin slammed his book shut and threw it down on the bed. Anger and determination had taken over. He went swiftly to the closet, got out the knapsack and umbrella, hoisted the knapsack onto his back and put his arms through the straps. Then he slammed the closet door shut with all of his might, unsnapped the umbrella, unfurled it, and opened it up until it clicked.

"To my tree in the forest," he said.

The umbrella remained suspended in midair for a split second and then dropped to the bedroom floor.

ELEVEN

DEEPER INTO THE FOREST

"I know," said Crispin, looking miserably at Greyfell, "I don't have the umbrella."

His realization of what he had done had been simultaneous with its effect. There was no possible way of retrieving it without jeopardizing the entire quest.

"Might one ask where it is?" Greyfell spoke gently. He could see that the boy was very troubled and embarrassed and felt very sorry for him but, like opening a boil, he thought it would be better to lance it and get everything out.

"It's in my room. The door is locked. But Tarquin always comes through the bathroom, anyway. You can only lock that door from the bathroom side."

"How did you happen to leave it behind?"

"I had an argument with my mother. She wanted me to promise never to come here again and when I wouldn't she locked me in my room. I got very angry and . . . Oh! Greyfell, I'm so very sorry. I wasn't thinking . . . and now . . . ." Here Crispin broke down at last. He had been over-excited and under a strain for hours. Now the frustration and grief poured out: he would fail in the quest, the tree would die, his parents wouldn't understand *anything* and would be very angry and send him away to an orphanage or a reformatory, and . . . .

"Things that are meant to work out will work themselves out," Greyfell said wisely. "Provided, of course, we do what we can to help." He paused and cleared his throat. That didn't seem to be coming out quite right. He started again, "Sometimes the mistakes we make turn out to be for the best." That sounded better, so he cleared his throat again. "And furthermore . . ."

"But we won't have the umbrella on the quest and we may need it to get back in time from . . . wherever we're going."

"An objection well-taken: but one which in no way invalidates my own thesis." Greyfell's voice had taken on a magisterial tone and he felt that a pair of spectacles to gesture with might add weight to his line of argument. Crispin surprised him by saying, abruptly, "You're trying to make me feel better. Thank you." He pulled out his big watch, clicked open the lid, saw that it was going on eleven already, and asked, "Where's Malgrin?"

"Falcons are so swift I expected him back before you. They are also immensely intelligent and clever, so he should be here momentarily. They too are given to rages at times . . . What is that little plate you have in your hand?"

"It's a watch. Haven't you seen a watch before? But of course you wouldn't have, how could you?" Crispin began to explain to the wolf how the watch told time when Malgrin seemed to materialize effortlessly on a nearby branch.

"I'm late. I'm sorry. I ran into a confabulation of crows and had the devil of a time giving them the slip. Troublesome birds! But not stupid: That's what makes it so tricky. They do have a way of collecting their entire tribe within seconds, and I had to go way out of my way before I could lose them and then double back, on the QT as it were. And it took me forever to run the young man to earth, a task better suited to hounds than to birds on the wing . . . although we do have the advantage of altitude. My message is that we are to meet tomorrow morning at the east bridge at 6:00. It's the best we could work out."

The wolf looked at Crispin who looked down at his feet. Then the wolf looked up at Malgrin and looked back at the boy.

"Something is not right here," said the falcon. "What is it?"

Crispin looked up at Greyfell and then at Malgrin and said, "I left the umbrella at home; a thoughtless mistake. I'm sorry,"

Malgrin shrugged, "Well, since the rendezvous is not until six tomorrow morning, perhaps you have just time enough to go back and get it, since you'll only have to walk one way."

"I don't think I can do that," Crispin explained. "You see, I was locked in my room. I was being punished for . . . because I wouldn't obey my mother. By this time Tarquin will have discovered that I'm not *in* my room, and if . . ."

"Ah, I see," Malgrin nodded. "You're absolutely right. Let us forget all about the umbrella for the time being. I could never use it anyway. And we should certainly be able to keep the appointment without it. Since I do very little walking myself, I will turn this part of the planning session over to Greyfell."

"Well, my young friend, how accustomed are you to hiking long distances?"

"I suppose I'm not really used to it. When I go any distance I usually ride my bike. I play in the woods a lot, and climb trees, but I don't get very far from home. And anyway, my stride is not very long because . . . well . . . because my legs . . ."

"Perhaps they'll stretch as we go along," interrupted the wolf, realizing they were approaching a tender subject. There's nothing like a good, stretching walk to help develop your stride."

"How far do we have to go?"

"That's a fair question, but difficult," said the wolf. "You measure distances by what you call *miles*, I believe, but we measure by time. At an ordinary wolf pace it takes me about two and a half to three hours. Difficult to judge: not having a watch."

Crispin looked puzzled. "What's the 'wolf pace'?" he asked.

"Well, you know, it's loping for a while, and then jog-trotting for about the same while, and then loping again. It eats up distances pretty quickly, but clearly we can't use it on this trip. I suggest we get started so that we can go at an easy pace with plenty of time for rest periods as needed."

"And if you don't mind," put in Malgrin, I will ride on your shoulder from time to time and help keep you company."

"But, where exactly are we going?" Crispin asked as he slung his knapsack over his shoulder. "And who are we going to meet?"

"Before I answer that, and before we forget it, let me put the scroll in your knapsack."

Crispin unslung his knapsack and took the scroll from Greyfell. He reread it carefully, trying to commit it to memory and being quite successful. (He memorized things often, sometimes not even being aware of what he was doing.) Then he tied the scroll carefully in the pocket beneath the flap of the knapsack Greyfell surveyed the entire platform out of which rose the great tree, and they set off down the steps on the opposite side from which Crispin had first come.

Before he went down the steps however, the boy turned back a few paces and looked up. The enormous trunk rose straight up until it was obscured by branch after branch with spreading clouds of pine needles, and the light that filtered down through them, although it was still the strong noonday sun, seemed to Crispin like starlight, like the oldest light in the universe, spent, exhausted by its journey. Even as he looked up he could feel dead needles falling about him. A lump swelled in his throat and he clenched his fists and said aloud, "I will. I will do this. God help me!" Then he turned, and started down.

At the bottom of the steps a wide track led off into the forest and Crispin remembered what his mother had said about the forest being a dangerous place and that he was not to go there and his heart sank more than a little as he contemplated the magnitude of his disobedience. He tried to put it out of his mind.

"About the bridges," he prompted Greyfell.

"Yes, of course. There are *two* bridges, the east bridge and the west bridge. There *were* some in between, but they don't count. The west bridge is the one you discovered, quite by accident, it seems (if anything happens *quite* by accident), and the east bridge lies almost directly opposite, as the crow flies (I beg your pardon, Malgrin; merely a figure of speech.) on the other side of the forest."

"And beyond that, we hope, lies the solution to the riddles and the salvation of the tree," added Malgrin.

"Exactly so."

"And who built the bridges? And who built the steps? And cleared this cart track?"

"Ah. Well. That was all done a long, long time before I was born."

"But you must know," Crispin persisted. "Your family has lived in this forest for ages, haven't they? Your grandfather must have told you, if you thought to ask."

"My grandfather was an extraordinarily wise old wolf and probably the world's best tracker, but he was also very close-mouthed when he wished to be."

"Malgrin, surely your family has been here for long enough to know all the forest's secrets. It can't be so deep a mystery that *you* wouldn't know!"

"Technically, we are not *forest* birds at all. As *raptores* (I use the official Latin label for the sake of accuracy) our domain is the cliff, the field and farmyard where we can see the slightest movement from very high up. We also hunt in the purlieus of the forest, it is true, but that hardly gives one access to its secrets."

"And the young man that we are going to meet, can you, or *will* you, tell me anything about him?"

The wolf paused in his walk and thought. "Let him introduce himself; I think that would be best. But . . ."

Crispin began to realize that his two friends were very reluctant to give him any information, and just the thinnest thread of doubt began to work its way through his confidence in both the falcon and the wolf. Could it be that they were drawing him deeper and deeper into the forest for some dreadful purpose of their own? Could it be that his mother was right after all?

" . . . I can tell you that he is twenty-four and . . .""Twenty-four! I thought you said he was young!" . . . knows as much about the forest, its trails, tracks, haunts, and glades as any man now living. Is twenty-four not young? And he drives an automobile."

"Does it have a rumble-seat?"

"A rumble-seat? I have no idea; I have never seen it, or any automobile. Malgrin, does it have a rumble-seat?"

"It does not. At least, not as I understand the term. A rumble-seat is that sort of open cockpit in the rear, correct?"

"Yes."

"Then it has no rumble-seat. Is that bad?"

"My father's car has one; I love riding in it." The thought of his father and the rumble-seat reminded Crispin of the home he was leaving further and further behind with every step he took. It was not only his father and mother, but Tarquin and baby Justin and Yettie and that did it. He stopped.

"I'm hungry, he said.

"I have been waiting for you to say that for quite a while now. If you can wait just a bit longer I think I can promise you a running stream and a mossy bank." And, naturally, the wolf was right.

TWELVE

THE LEOPARD

They had been walking for so long that Crispin began to wonder whether he had been born walking and would never be able to stop in this life. His feet began to bother him because of the irregularities in the track. His legs followed suit. The sun had set but, because of the tall trees, they had been walking in darkness long before it went down. Slowly, silently, the moon rose, but its effect was only to make the darkness deeper by contrast with its silvering light. Nevertheless, the broad track was always clear before them, rising around hills or descending into hollows, no longer with flights of steps, but once it crossed a stone bridge, a smaller version of the disappearing bridge whose secret Crispin had discovered.

They had stopped once so that Crispin could finish off anything that was left in his knapsack and empty the thermos. The remaining squares of chocolate he wrapped up again in their foil and put them in his pocket. Greyfell refused to touch anything. "My eating habits have always been irregular, but not yours, I suspect. So, thank you just the same, but don't worry about me."

Malgrin had disappeared somewhere to roost, promising to catch up with them in the morning. Crispin trudged onwards, beginning to fall asleep even as he walked. "Stop!" Greyfell whispered a command. The boy stopped mechanically. They had come to the edge of an enormous clearing; the track led straight across it, but he was hardly aware of the clearing until the wolf said quietly, "Look there."

Crispin looked in the direction indicated and drew in a quick, startled breath. A long, grey stone building loomed in the center of the clearing, given extra height because it was supported on a high terrace. In its center was a squat, square tower, and the building stretched out on either side in three rows of windows: pairs of lancet windows at the bottom, large mullioned windows above, and, along the edge of the roof, a row of identical dormer windows. The moon glittered in a pane or two so that Crispin felt he was trying to see the eyes of somebody wearing spectacles in the sunlight.

"This is the most dangerous part of our journey; how I wish there were no moon tonight."

"What on earth is it?" breathed Crispin.

"It is the Abbey that owned . . . *owns* the forest," explained Greyfell. It has been empty ever since . . . for longer than I know. Now it is inhabited by the Leopard of Tryce. We have to cross in front of it and whether he has sentinels posted, well, there's only one way to find out. Too bad Malgrin flew off to roost, he might have scouted. But it makes no difference since cross we must. Now, if we hurry too much we will surely attract attention and if we move too slowly it will take us forever, so let us simply continue at the pace we have been going. But make no sound."

The boy was now wide awake, and questions jostled one another in his brain, but Crispin the Indian Scout was used to moving noiselessly; questions he could ask later. And so they started off: a quarter of the way across and no trouble; at half-way the track led close under the terrace wall—still no trouble; three quarters and still nothing.

Suddenly a long, shrill whistle sounded above them, the kind of whistle you make by sticking two fingers between your teeth. Then, barely audible, the tinkling of a silvery bell sounded once and was silent. The two walkers pushed forward at a brisker pace and, just as they left the clearing and plunged back into the deep shadows, Crispin glanced back over his shoulder for one last look. He thought he saw a light behind one of the large windows, and he was going to mention it to the wolf but decided not to. *It may be only the moonlight,* he thought.

*

Crispin's knees buckled under him and he snapped awake. The excitement of the Abbey in its clearing had kept him awake for almost an hour but it could not last. He walked asleep and walked *in* his sleep until his knees gave out.

"Well, my young friend," said Greyfell, "you need sleep. You have kept the pace well and I think we can afford two or three hours. And it might be a very good idea to get off the track for awhile."

Crispin hauled out his grandfather's watch and clicked open the lid. His pupils were wide open from walking through the nighttime forest and, with a trickle of moon-beam to assist; he could just make out the time—2:35! He had never been up this late before. Not even on Christmas Eve when he had tried to stay awake to see Santa Claus. That was three years ago when he had fallen asleep well before midnight and Tarquin had claimed that Santa had arrived only a short time later and he hadn't entirely believed his brother, who

was consistently on top of situations or trying to keep the upper hand and . . . .
His knees buckled again.

"Come along. Just follow me." The wolf left the track, picking his way carefully among roots of the great trees so that the boy could follow easily through the ferns and around saplings, and steadily up a slope. Shortly they came to a shallow pocket lined with soft grasses, mosses, and dried ferns that almost seemed made for small boys to sleep out of doors. He let his knapsack slide off his shoulders and was himself asleep before he was fully on the ground.

Sleeping out of doors, when you first start doing it, is rarely very deep, but Crispin's was not only deep but tenacious. Nevertheless, a long, quiet growl eventually worked its way into his deepest dreams. Then, at a slightly higher level, he heard a jingle and a clink. Higher still and nearly awake, he felt that something was placing footprints into the pine needles of the track. Then he was fully awake and sat up. But a great paw pushed him gently down again into the ferns, and "Shhhhh," breathed Greyfell so softly that Crispin was not sure that he hadn't thought it himself. "Listen."

He heard again the jingling clink, and it reminded him of the teams of horses on the road outside his gate at home. He recognized that what he thought he could feel were the hoof-prints of horses, but infinitely more quiet and delicate than the big, jingling draft horses on his own road. Greyfell growled again, softly and deeply, and Crispin could feel the hair standing up on the wolf's back as, "Look," he breathed again.

Slowly, ever so cautiously, the boy raised his head. Down the slope in front of them, between the trees, he could see a stretch of the track along which they had come. The thin light of the declining moon fell onto the track and there, coming towards them, rode three men on horseback. To Crispin they looked as though they had just ridden out of his King Arthur story book. They were not strapped into armor, although there was a glint of steel about the man in the lead. The boy recognized the style of their clothing and his eyes grew as round as teacups.

The man in the lead wore no hat or hood, but around his temples was a thin circlet of gold that fit so closely it looked as though he could never take it off, and perhaps he never did. His jagged sleeves swept down below the belly of his horse. Most amazing of all, straining like hounds at the ends of two leashes, were two spotted leopards. Underneath the chin of each leopard, on a collar around its neck, was a tiny silver bubble of a bell. When they rang they made the high, tinkling sound that Crispin had already heard that night. The two leopards made the horse nervous and it arched it neck and shook its harness, making the jingling noise that had worked its way into Crispin's dreams.

Crispin stared again. "It's my leopard," he said in a hoarse whisper, that is, the leopard he had met high in the great tree.

The rider in front stopped immediately, as did the others after him. He raised his head and looked in their direction and Crispin saw something that made his heart turn over, and his blood freeze. The rider's eyes blazed with an incandescent light, as indeed the eyes of the other two blazed and, worse, the eyes of the horses did as well, as though each horse and rider was empty of everything inside except a furnace. The boy felt that this blazing light could find him wherever he was.

The rider raised his voice, "Are you there, my young enemy?"

The voice, too, was hollow, empty though deep and it seemed to flicker around the edges, or rasp.

Crispin was silent.

"Find!" commanded the rider, and he leaned way over and unsnapped the leash from one of the leopards. Greyfell's fur bristled: he bared his lethal teeth and crouched to spring. Like lightning the leopard took the slope but stopped, almost suspended in mid-spring. "Hel—lo!" she said, "it's the boy with the peanut butter sandwiches."

"But: . . . what a surprise to see *you* again!" Crispin stood up spontaneously. "I recognized you immediately."

"I'm equally surprised to see you, and in such unsavory company, too." Here the leopard responded to the wolf with snarl for snarl.

"How did you get off your courthouse roof?" asked Crispin, trying to distract the leopard. He dreaded having a cat-and-dog-fight on his hands.

"It's really a question of appearance and reality: some other time." The leopard eyed the knapsack expectantly. "You don't by any chance have one of those delicious sandwiches in your knapsack?"

"I'm sorry, but I don't."

"No, I was afraid not."

"I didn't make the sandwiches myself this time. Next time I'll be sure to bring some extras. But I have some chocolate left." He reached into his pocket for the remaining squares of chocolate, removed the foil, and held them out on the palm of his hand.

"Is this anything like peanut butter?"

"No, but it should go very well with peanut butter, I would think, although I've never tried it."

Then the squares were gone. "Emmmmmm," purred the leopard, "something else that clings to your teeth. Where do you get these goodies?"

Before Crispin could say anything, a harsh command rasped up from the track below. "Return!"

"O fiddle-Dee Dee," sniffed the leopard, "my Master's voice. Return I must, it is the law. Thank you so much for the snack; he keeps us hungry most of the time."

"But tell me your name this time, please, before you go."

"I have no name. The Master refuses to give us names, just commands. It's part of his power." And the leopard turned and sprang down the slope before the command had to be repeated. Crispin and Greyfell both stood and watched as the man clipped the leopard back onto its leash. In guttural undertones he said something to the leopard and even raised a threatening fist, making the leopard try to shrink away, although he still held onto its collar.

"It's the Leopard of Tryce," Greyfell growled in his throat.

"Which one?"

"No, no. Not the cats. Him! The Leopard of Tryce."

"Oh," the boy whispered. "It was *his* seal, the Leopard."

"Precisely," said the wolf.

Below them on the track the Leopard of Tryce raised his head and stood up in his stirrups. His baleful gaze swept towards them like twin searchlights so that both the boy and the wolf dropped down beneath the lip of the hollow.

"Hear me, my young enemy," blazed that voice. "You think you will win because you are young and smart. You think you will win and save the tree, but, young as you are, you will run out of time. I'll see to that. You *will* run out of time. And as for that wolf . . ." He finished with a snarl worthy of any leopard. He whirled his horse, causing consternation among the two retainers behind him and almost strangling the leopards in their leashes, and all three riders galloped back down the track.

There was silence in the forest.

"I didn't know I had an enemy," said Crispin at last. "How did I get an enemy? Or why? And who *is* he?"

"It's the Leopard of Tryce: The Archduke of Tryce. He owns . . . *owned* this entire county and more . . . . except for the forest. He always wanted the forest. He has been dead for several hundreds of years."

"Dead!" Crispin felt his scalp crawl and felt ice form along his backbone and a hollow open behind both knees. With difficulty he controlled his voice as he asked, "Greyfell, what have I gotten myself into? I wish Tarquin were here, he would know what to do."

"Crispin," admonished the wolf, "remember that the dead can never *really* hurt you. Frighten you? Yes. But not hurt. You are doing splendidly so far, and you are just the person, the only person, to save the great tree."

"The tree, the tree, I was forgetting my tree! Come on! He said I would run out of time. Let's go. Greyfell, come on!"

He thrust his hand into his pocket and pulled out the big watch but Greyfell put his paw gently over the boy's trembling hand. "Crispin: sometimes haste makes waste. You have had an experience few other boys have ever had; you are wide awake and have gone with very little sleep for going on twenty-four hours. Put the watch away. We can start to walk again if you like. You probably cannot do anything else, and the track will be empty now. But as soon as you start to fall asleep again, we'll stop."

They did that. And Crispin slept.

THIRTEEN

THE YOUNG MAN

The young man kept his eyes trained across the bridge on the place where the track emerged from the trees. Nor had he been watching long before Crispin and Greyfell came down the track towards the bridge, the boy taking long determined strides (for a small boy) and the wolf at his side. The young man glanced at his watch and smiled, "Remarkable. Six o'clock on the nose."

*

Earlier, when Crispin had awakened with a start, everything still seemed plunged in darkness. Huddled into his blue sweater, he was about to roll over when he noticed the shapes of trees beginning to show against the paling sky. He scrambled to his feet to find Greyfell already up and regarding the sky himself. Crispin could not quite remember sinking into the cradle of roots by the side of the track; he had slept without taking off his knapsack so he was ready to set off at once. There were pine needles in his hair and stuck into his sweater and even one down his back; his face was smudged and there was sleep in the corners of his eyes. "Good morning, Greyfell, my legs ache. How does the day look?"

"Good morning, Crispin. What a walker you are! Your legs will be fine after a little more walking. The day may turn out even better than yesterday, once this ground mist clears off. What does your watch say?"

Crispin checked the watch, "Five-thirty. Can it be morning already?" he asked, as they set off down the track.

"The summer sun must be up already, on the other side of this hill. We haven't too much further to go and most of it downhill. And we'll get some breakfast into you as soon as we can. How are your feet and legs now?"

"Better, now that I'm walking. What has become of Malgrin?"

"He may be breakfasting even now, but don't worry, he will catch up in no time, when he's ready."

They walked on in silence. Crispin had questions that he wanted to ask about last night's episode with the Leopard of Tryce and his horsemen, but Greyfell had indicated that answers would come later. As they topped the rise the sun shone full in their faces for a minute until the track bent again. The local birds were up, an occasional squirrel whisked out of sight as they approached, and in the far distance Crispin could hear crows. He hoped they were not mobbing Malgrin; they didn't *sound* angry so that was all right. Still they walked and walked and the boy became increasingly aware of his empty, growling stomach, and still they walked. He started to drowse; his walk became a shamble, and then almost a stumble, and suddenly he could see the end of the trees, and once more he was wide awake.

On the other side of the bridge, stood a very large Pierce Arrow touring car: it glistened silvery-green in the slanting sunlight as though it had just been polished and buffed, or had just been transplanted direct from the showroom. Spare tires stood on either side of its long hood, the front fenders flowed towards the back, developing into long running-boards before curling over the rear tires and beneath the rear window was a large trunk that opened from the top.

Next to the automobile stood the young man "of twenty-four years." He had an interesting, triangular sort of face, with a very narrow, closely trimmed beard and mustache under a nose almost too small for his face. He wore a light flannel suit, a white shirt and striped tie, and a soft hat to keep the sun out of his eyes. On the other side of the Pierce Arrow stood a very old, untrimmed, moth-eaten (one would say) green bay tree.

Crispin had already started across the bridge when he heard the wolf's voice behind him: "Well, this is as far as I go." The boy turned and saw that Greyfell had stopped, just short of the bridge. He went back.

"But you can't stop now! I'll need your advice and your strength. I don't know *anything* about what I'm doing, but you do."

"No. I am the custodian of the forest, or at least of what goes on underneath its trees. I can't do much about what goes on *in* its branches (witness the witch), but I cannot leave it either. I've reached my limit."

"I will miss you."

"It can't be helped. Besides, we will see each other again before sundown, I hope."

From the top of the bridge he watched the great grey wolf lope up the track and into the trees. "Greyfell, wait!" He had only just remembered something. "Greyfell, I want to ask you about my mother and father. They know . . ." But the wolf was gone.

He looked up into the sky and raised his voice, "Malgrin, Malgrin, come bird!" and held up his fist. Up in the highest blue, the falcon folded its wings and dropped. At the last moment it braked with its wings and lit gently on the up-stretched fist.

"We've lost Greyfell!" exclaimed the boy, "and he left before I could ask him about my mother and father. They seem to know everything about the forest. I overheard them accidentally. What can that mean? This is all such a muddle . . . we saw the Leopard of Tryce last night and he called me 'his enemy,' and I won't know which way to turn, and . . . ." He lowered his arm and the falcon flicked its wings and perched on the boy's shoulder to be closer to his ear.

"Now youngster, listen to me." Malgrin spoke quietly but huskily into his ear, but spoke with authority, too. "Wolves live far longer than falcons and Greyfell's memory is very long indeed. My family told me nothing except how to plunge and strike, and I think I knew that, anyway. I have been set aside to assist you. I am dedicated to that. Now, turn around and go forward. There is one who is waiting."

And so, without looking back, but with a disappointed heart, Crispin turned and finished crossing the bridge toward the car and its waiting attendant.

"Good morning, young Master. My name is Blight."

"My name is Crispin. Good morning." He stuck out his hand and they shook "Is Blight your first name or your last?"

"It is what I am called, young Master; and good morning, Malgrin."

"Oh. Well, my name is *not* young Master, so I'll call you Blight if you call me Crispin."

"It goes hard," said Blight, with a twinkle in his eye, "but I'll try. Now Crispin [said very deliberately], you look like a young man who has just spent a night in the forest. You need a wash and comb and breakfast and I think I know just the place."

"Couldn't I have them the other way around?" he asked. He had been so long without food that his head had begun to ache, although he only just realized that.

"We'll see. Get in quickly, and why don't you let me lock your knapsack in the trunk for safe-keeping?"

"Excuse me, Malgrin, but I have to get these straps off my shoulders. Will you fly? Or ride with me?"

"I'll fly and keep a lookout and, who knows? Perhaps I'll do a little hunting. I could do with some breakfast myself." With a flick of wing and tail, Malgrin was gone and only the faintest cry of We *chew* drifted down from high above.

Crispin unslung his knapsack and carried it to the rear of the car and watched while Blight locked it in the trunk. Then he climbed into the front seat (the running board was quite high, even for a boy of seven) and sank into the wonderfully comfortable upholstery. He had never been in a car so big; the back seat seemed miles away, and the radiator cap on the front of the hood equally far away. "Where are we going?" he asked.

"Not far. In fact, you can just see it from here." And he nodded in the direction of a grove of trees and rooftops and chimneys that Crispin had not noticed before. By this time Blight had the motor humming so quietly that one had to pay attention to hear it at all. Then he leaned out of his open window and picked two leaves from the green bay tree and stuck the stem of one into his mouth. He shifted into gear and they rolled forward. The other leaf he slid into his inside breast pocket.

"Why did you do that?"

"Do what?"

"Pick those leaves?" The boy was thinking of his own experience with leaves from bay tees.

"Turn around and look."

"I only see the bridge and the forest."

"Exactly. The bridge should disappear once the last human is out of the forest and across the bridge. I have prevented that by pulling off two leaves. As long as the bridge stands we will be able to understand our friend, Malgrin. Otherwise . . ."

Crispin, having spent much of the night hiking rather than sleeping, lost track of what his companion was saying and, although he was sure he hadn't missed a word, was already asleep.

Blight was following the traces of an ancient roadway, so faint that you would never see it unless you knew exactly where to look. Blight knew. In fact, so well did he know the track that he hardly had to pay attention at all. They rode across a vast meadow dappled with cows that were themselves dappled brown and white; they dipped once through the ford of a shallow stream and came up on the other side with wheels dripping; they ran through the shade of giant oak and elm, turned the corner of a long, stone wall, passed through an open gate, and drove into a cobbled yard so big and surrounded on every side by so many workshops and sheds, cottages, barns, byres, and even a substantial house, that it looked more like a village square that a farmyard. But it had a flock of white geese that paraded across the yard in a formation recognized only by themselves. Everything was built of stone, very much like Crispin's own house, and looked tremendously old, mellow, and sun-bleached, with shades of grey and palest shades of stony pinks and yellows and blues showing here and there. Some few of the buildings were open to the elements, their roofs having fallen in many years ago, but most were in excellent repair.

The silvery-green Pierce Arrow rolled gently to a stop by the substantial house. Blight would have liked to let the boy sleep but there was no time for sleep now—clocks don't stop while people sleep. Blight went to the door of the house that gave onto the yard, opened it and leaned in. "Mother," he called, "Here's young Agincroft."

Shortly, Crispin was plunging his face and hands into warm, soapy water in a low sink. Boiling hot water had been supplied from a large kettle by Blight's mother, and this had been tempered by cold water from the pump at the sink. The boy, with eyes tightly shut against the soap, groped for the towel placed on the drain-board. He rubbed and dried, and then combed his hair as well as he could with no mirror and no comb. Up two stone steps he went into what seemed to him a vast kitchen, and found breakfast spread out on a large, round wooden table with a stool placed for him and a chair for Blight.

But even before he climbed onto the stool, Crispin glanced around the kitchen, looking for a clock. He found a small steeple clock on a shelf over a dresser; 7:03 it read. He glanced at Blight who narrowed his eyes and nodded, as much as to say, "Have no fear; there will be time." Then the boy attacked breakfast.

Blight's mother stood ready to supply more, should it be required, and watched with approval as Crispin demolished what was set before him. He said very little during breakfast except an occasional "Yes please," or "No, thank you." Somewhere in the middle of bacon and eggs he stopped eating, lifted his head and turned to the window. The geese were making a noisy racket of hissing and honking.

"I don't know what's gotten into those geese," said Mrs. Blight, putting down two more slices of toast beside Crispin's plate. "They've been gabbling all morning as though there were a wildcat in the neighborhood."

But the boy had heard a 'jingle and clink' that he recognized immediately, and he had *felt*, rather than heard, hoof prints on the cobblestones that made the hair on the back of his neck rise. He glanced at Blight, who kept his head down but lifted one eyebrow. He glanced at Mrs. Blight, but she had obviously heard only the geese. He returned to his breakfast but kept an eye peeled on the window. Nothing passed.

At length he was mopping up the last of his fried eggs with a piece of bread and wondering whether he should sneak a lick of his fingers. He decided against that, and used the big napkin spread over his lap.

Just as Crispin finished breakfast another man came into the kitchen. He was shorter than Blight but looked rock-solid and the boy saw at once that it must be Blight's father, as indeed it was.

"You must be young Agincroft; Crispin is it?" He extended a hardened but shapely hand.

"Yes, sir," said the boy springing off his stool. "And you must be Mister . . . Blight?" They shook hands.

"Right you are. Good grip, too." With his foot he hooked a chair up to the table and sat down; then he said abruptly, "Now about these riddles."

Mrs. Blight turned away from the sink where she had started washing up breakfast and stood behind her husband's chair drying a bowl. All three looked expectantly at the boy, who said, "The scroll is in my knapsack in the trunk of the car. But I think I can do the riddles from memory."

"Good lad," said Blight's father. "That's what I like, no nonsense. Well?"

Mrs. Blight put her hand gently on her husband's shoulder while Crispin shut his eyes and pressed them with his fingertips for concentration. Then he recited:

> "From the destruction of the broom: seven days.
> But only seven years will win it.
> Whether in water, earth, air, or fire,
> Whether in all or none of these
> That the second broom ye shall recover,
> I doubt."

"Malgrin says they've tried all of that, run to earth, air, and water too, every lead they could think of, hear of, or suspect," this from Blight. "They would do a completely thorough job, I think."

"Yes they would," insisted Mrs. Blight.

"All right: There must be more. What's next?"

Again the boy knitted his brows and pressed his eyelids closed.

> "Failing this:
> Try across the Wider Water;
> Longshanks, he the hamper has.
> Try to find the Black Witch Blood;
> From that a new direction take,
> Learning as ye go along
> To have done
> With my forest."

"Did I get that right?" He looked around for Greyfell, and remembered. Then there was silence in the kitchen. The clock on its shelf ticked noisily. The boy held his breath. He had been depending on the grey wolf to give him some sort of lead, since the riddles meant nothing that he could even begin to guess at.

"Longshanks: Longshanks. There's a Longshanks over in the next county, I think; a huge estate with a strange history. I hear about it occasionally at market. Not doing too well, I think I heard. Let's get out the map." Before his father could move, Blight was at the dresser under the clock, rummaging through its top drawer. He came back unfolding a large map which he spread out on the table. His mother rescued the sugar bowl and moved the salt and pepper shakers.

"Come around here, Crispin, by me," Mr. Blight directed, and made room at the foot of the map. "Now, here we are, just here," he said, tapping the map with his finger, "at Priorfields. This is the forest," a vast stretch of green. The boy wanted to examine the other side of the forest for his own home, but put that thought out of his mind. "And, over here—the next county: just beyond the river here, is, yes, the village, and . . . ah! There it is, Longshanks." Again he tapped the map.

"The closest bridge is way around by Tryceholdings," said Blight, likewise tapping the map.

"But look here!" Crispin was a map-fanatic, and had quickly focused on Longshanks. "Look, this little dotted line, shouldn't that mean there's a ferry here?"

"He's right." Blight looked at his father. "I remember it now; I think it's called the "Wider Water Ferry."

"Holy Casmittima! Then we must be on the right track there. 'Try across the Wider Water.' Come on, may we get started? Please?"

FOURTEEN

ROADBLOCK

The pace of activity in the kitchen changed suddenly. Mrs. Blight sliced bread from various loaves and put together a variety of sandwiches, wrapping each in wax paper.

Crispin requested, "Peanut butter and jelly, too, please, Mrs. Blight? I've made a promise." But he did not mention to whom the promise had been made. Instead, he took out his grandfather's watch and checked the time against the steeple clock, wound the watch carefully, and restored it to his pocket. Then he rejoined Blight and his father, who had their heads together over the map, plotting the quickest route to the ferry.

"If you try to go through Chewing Cud you'll find it's market day," Mr. Blight was saying. That could slow you way down. But if you take this lane here, it will put you in the Trudgefurrow farmyard. Old man Trudge will let you use his cart track. (Just tell him who you are.) It runs along here and into this lane, and that will put you back on the county road."

"How long will this take us, Dad?"

"It's what? 8:35 now. You should reach the ferry before noon. Easily, I would say."

The four of them came out to the waiting automobile, Mrs. Blight carrying a small basket packed with edibles, Blight folding up the map "in case," and Crispin, looking up, thought he could just see a falcon navigating the air currents high above.

"Let me get my sneakers out of my duffel, and then I can take these high tops off as we drive."

The sneakers rescued, Mrs. Blight discovered the thermos bottle and took it inside to rinse out and refill with fresh milk. As if by magic, or at a signal, a few workmen started to emerge from shops and stables and waved their caps and hats as Blight started the engine and rolled the car easily forward.

They had come into the great yard by the back way, but now they left it through massive gates supported on both sides by stone pillars. Over the center of the arch, on the outside, was a large shield that was supported on either side by a wolf. They sped off down the lane that led from the gates, sped between rows of beech and linden trees. Crispin fell to removing his high tops and substituting the sneakers, but looking up repeatedly as though he were memorizing the route they were taking, until . . .

"Blight?"

"Yes, Crispin."

"During breakfast . . . . You heard that sound during breakfast?"

"What sound was that?"

"Oh, come on, I could tell you heard it: the sound of horses . . . . just after the geese started up."

"Yes, I did hear it."

"But your mother didn't."

"She wouldn't let on, even if she did."

"That was the Leopard of Tryce."

"Yes."

"I could tell by the sound, exactly the same as I heard in the forest last night. But this morning I didn't see anything."

"Ah. You heard that last night. And did you *see* anything then?"

"Yes." The boy turned and looked steadily at his companion. "You've seen the Leopard too."

The driver smiled a grim smile. "I have that. Not a cheerful sight."

"Tell me about him, will you please? Nobody else will."

"I don't know everything." (Crispin drew in his breath between his teeth and shook his head in frustration.) "But I will tell you whatever I can. The Tryce family was very ancient, very distinguished, and *very* powerful. Now the county seat in Tryceholdings is all that's left of what used to be their stronghold, a vast stone hive of bees or hornets, depending on your point of view. At the center of the family was the Archduke. He owned everything and ran everything, *every*thing except . . ."

"The forest."

" . . . and its farms, meadows and fields."

"That must be your place, Blight?"

"Yes: Priorfields, but not really *ours*. My family has maintained it for generations . . . but it belongs to the Abbey."

Blight slowed down as they approached a crossroads, and suddenly Crispin cried, "Look!" On a branch arching over the middle of the road sat the peregrine falcon. Brakes applied, the automobile came to a standstill and they both got out.

"Might one ask *where* we are going?" asked Malgrin, somewhat sourly, from his branch.

"I'm so sorry, Malgrin; I couldn't tell whether that was you way up there or not."

"Well, since my eyes are keener than yours, next time just stick out your left arm and wave with your right. You will know soon enough."

Here Blight interposed, "It was probably my fault, your honor, but it won't happen again. Now, we think we have located Longshanks on the other side of the Wider Water where the river grows, inevitably . . . [Here he shrugged his shoulders.] . . . wider. A very large place, Longshanks, plagued with some difficulties recently. That would be about thirty miles from here, south and a little east."

"The territory is unknown to me, but I think I have a cousin or two in that direction. Consider us an advance scouting party. Did you see the horsemen go through Priorfields?"

"No. I couldn't see them, but I heard them, and Blight did too. Were there three?"

"I couldn't see them in the sunlight, either; only when they passed through deep shadows. I fear they are heading in the same direction we are."

"The only thing they can hope to do," Blight reminded them, "is to slow us down so that we run out of time. Therefore, Malgrin, if you will assemble your Advance Scouting Party, Crispin and I will make as speedy progress as possible over these country lanes."

With only a flutter and a flash, the falcon was gone. The other two returned to the car and were soon racing down the narrow roads, for all the world like a cross-country motor rally. After waiting a polite length of time, the boy suggested, "You were telling me about the Leopard of Tryce."

"Ah yes. Well. What had once been a great family began to *shrink*, I suppose we could say, until, in the final generation, there were just two brothers left plus a rumored, improbable, illegitimate third. After the old Archduke died, the elder brother, Blaise, gave up his title and all of his vast inheritance to the younger and entered the Abbey in the forest. In the course of time he became the Abbot, whereas the younger brother, Axel, moving in quite the opposite direction, took to wicked, grasping, greedy, and violent ways and ultimately came to be called the 'Leopard of Tryce.' I believe it was his brother who first called him that. At any rate, he never married and died childless."

"Was he very old when he died? He didn't seem old to me; but then, I wasn't very close, thank heaven. That was closer than I'd want to get."

"Quite the contrary, he was still young and vigorous, I believe, as people far older than I judge these things; somewhere in his thirties, his late thirties."

"But how did he die?"

"It was quite grizzly, according to the legend my mother told me. It seems he was returning to the Abbey after a day's hunting in the forest. He often went hunting completely alone, a sign, I'm told, of his arrogance. He turned for home as evening fell (when all good stories get better) and he began to hear the howl of wolves. Inevitably they drew closer. He was absolutely fearless himself but he knew that his horse was growing restless. He also knew that, of the two, his horse was more vulnerable than he, so he gave the horse its head and began to gallop like the wind for the Abbey. He didn't make it. His horse did; they found the animal in the stable yard still breathing heavily from its run and still trembling for quite another reason. They found the Leopard of Tryce at the foot of a gigantic tree, pulled from his horse, apparently, with most of his throat torn away but otherwise untouched.

"Strangest of all, sitting on its haunches next to the body was a giant grey wolf. The search party had come out with torches and weapons. They could just see the shape or shadow of the beast by the light of stars and moon, but its eyes flamed in the torchlight. The searchers fitted arrows to their bows but something kept them from shooting. The wolf remained stationary until they were practically on top of it and then, with a snarl, it sprang into the forest and disappeared."

Crispin sat silently, contemplating a world far more violent than his own, but one of which he had begun to catch glimpses.

"My mother used to remind me of the Leopard's fate when she thought I was getting too big for my britches . . . . a cautionary tale."

"But how did you happen to see the Leopard?"

"Don't think that didn't put the fear of God into me. I have never been so scared in my life, and hope never to be again. On that day I had gone deeper and deeper into the forest than I had ever been before, following paths and trails, cutting nicks in the bark of trees so that I could find my way out. I was trying to locate all the cells where the hermits used to live."

"Cells?" Crispin had visions of dungeons with dripping water and prisoners chained to walls.

"That's what they're called. Actually they are just very small stone cottages, but remarkably well-made with arched stone and slate roofs. Just one room with a fireplace and a window and a small garden attached, as it were. The hermit-monks who managed the forest lived in them, only returning to the Abbey for Sundays.

"By the time I realized how late it was I had a long way to go and it was pitch dark as I passed the big building. Mind, I had been in it and all through it in broad daylight and seen nothing. Now as I passed I heard a high, piercing whistle . . ."

"It must have been the same one we heard last night."

"Most likely it was. It made the hair stand up on my head and I started to run even faster than the jog-trot I had been doing. Not long afterwards I heard hoof-beats behind me. I knew I couldn't outrun horses so I took to the trees. I made a mighty great leap for an overhanging branch, scrambled up into a giant beech and swung around so that the trunk was between me and the track. And just in time, too, because three men on horseback went thundering beneath me. I was sure they would be back when they didn't find me ahead of them, so I climbed up higher and higher into the tree. My heart was pounding and I tried not to breathe so that I would make no noise.

"The night grew deathly quiet. Then I heard that jingle and clink, the same as we heard this morning. I looked down and could just make out the shape of them coming along the track with their strange searchlight eyes, and two leopards on long chains. I held my breath because they stopped beneath my tree. The one in the lead raised his voice: "Interloper, leave my forest and never return." It was the Leopard of Tryce, " . . . or suffer the consequences when I take you." Then they went off, back down the track.

"I waited and waited and finally climbed back down and dropped into the track and ran for the bridge like a champion."

"How long ago did that happen, Blight?"

"It must be seven years ago; I was just seventeen."

"But that didn't stop you from going back. Greyfell says you know more about the forest than he does."

"I doubt that but, no, it didn't stop me from going back. Things always look different by daylight. But I have always made sure to be out of the forest before dark."

"What I don't understand is how the Leopard can talk about the forest as *his* when it doesn't belong to him at all. It belongs to the Abbey, doesn't it?"

They had been zooming along between rows of trees, carefully avoiding farmer's carts and women on bicycles, and Blight said, "Well, of course it does, but—" He took his foot off of the accelerator and applied the brakes. "Was that Trudgefurrow Lane we just passed?"

"I'm sorry, I wasn't reading the signs. Should I have?"

"Not really. I know these roads *better* than the back of my hand (which I rarely look at); the problem comes from driving and talking at the same time." He shifted into reverse and backed quickly down the twenty-five or so yards to the corner. There was the narrow sign at the top of its post: "Trudgefurrow Lane."

"I was sure of it. How could I have missed it?" So they turned right into the lane and started to pick up speed again. The lane ran over a series of ridges and down into hollows so that speeding along it was something like riding a roller coaster until, coming over the highest ridge, they almost ran smack into a flock of sheep. Blight jammed on the brake and pulled the emergency brake at the same time. The Pierce Arrow skidded in the dirt of the lane and stopped just as the front bumper was beginning to lift the hind side of the nearest sheep. Then a whole exclamatory chorus of *baaas* arose from the flock.

In front of them the lane dipped down and ran the length of a long hollow with a hedgerow atop a bank on one side and a fence on the other. Between these two barriers the lane was packed solid with over a hundred sheep. Packed so solid they were, that Crispin felt he could walk over their backs without losing his footing or falling in. Blight put the car in reverse and backed a yard or two up the lane. At the other end of the hollow a young boy and a small, wildly barking dog kept the sheep from going in that direction. Half-way down, in the field on the other side of the fence, an older man had taken out the rails of a length of the fence and was trying to encourage the sheep to come into the field. They, on the other hand, seemed more inclined to go streaming up the lane on either side of the Pierce Arrow.

"Open your door!" directed Blight, opening his. That effectively blocked that exit for the flock; next he gave a few toots on the car horn. Then, with both the car and the young boy and barking dog pressing forward from either end, the middle of the flock bulged and started, at first in a trickle and then in a spate, to flow into the field. The boy and his dog advanced from one end; Blight and Crispin in the car advanced from the other, and the man in the middle got out of the way. By the time they reached the center of the hollow the last sheep had hurried into the field and the farmer was putting the rails back into the fence. Blight turned off the engine and got out. Crispin followed suit.

"You boys came along at just the right minute," said the farmer. "If those sheep had got up the lane we would have had quite a time getting them back. They might have been scattered half over the county. Lucky you came along."

"I'm Blight . . . *young* Blight from Priorfields," he said, sticking out his hand, "and you're Mr. Trudge, I think." They shook hands.

"Oh, ay, I know your father. Done more than a little business with Priorfields, from time to time; always a straight man to deal with, your father. This is my youngest boy, Hardy," with a pull of his chin in the direction of his son, who was older than Crispin, about Tarquin's age. "And the dog is Towser."

"Hello, Mr. Trudge, I'm young Agincroft from the other side of the forest. Pleased to meet you, Hardy." Hands were shaken all round.

"Can't imagine what got into those sheep," continued Mr. Trudge. "Something pretty near terrified them. All of a sudden they started running as though there was a pack of wolves or devils at their tails. But, funny, they didn't scatter as they ordinarily would. It was as though they'd been driven out into the lane and down here in the long dip and then stopped for a purpose. Unnatural, I call it. What brings you two down Trudgefurrow Lane?"

"We were trying to save time by not going through Chewing Cud on market day," the boy began, and Blight continued, "We planned to stop off and ask to use your cart track over to the county road."

"Well. I'm afraid you haven't saved much time at all, but you're more than welcome to use the track. Hardy, how many gates are open?"

"Only the first, I think, Dad."

"Just ride along with young Blight, here, if you don't mind, and do the gates for them. Towser can stay with me, can't you boy?"

"Thank you very much, sir," said Crispin shaking hands again.

"My father sends his best, and to the Missus," and Blight shook hands as well.

They got back into the car and Hardy closed the door behind Crispin and sprang onto the running board. He stuck his head in through the open window and said in a low voice, "Quick! Get moving before my dad makes me ride inside."

"Hardy, my boy, this is not a rodeo you're riding in," called his father. But he was too late. Only Towser ran along side barking, but he gave up the chase when Mr. Trudge called him back.

They drove carefully through the farmyard and waved to Mrs. Trudge where she was taking dry laundry off the lines and folding it into a big wicker basket. Hardy crouched down on the other side of the car so that his mother would not see him riding the running board.

As they approached each closed gate, Blight slowed the automobile to a crawl, Hardy jumped down and ran ahead, opened the gate and, as soon as the car was through, shut the gate except for a space he could get back through, caught up with the moving car and leapt back onto the running board. "I'll close them up on my way back," he said through the open window. Then they were off down the track to the next gate. Clockwork never ran better.

When they had passed through the last gate out onto the narrow county road, and after they had shouted and waved *Goodbye* to Hardy, who waved from behind the fence, Crispin turned to Blight and said, "About those sheep. I feel as though somebody has been reading our minds."

And Blight said, "Perhaps *someone* has."

FIFTEEN

BARGAINS, PRICES AND COST

Blight eased the Pierce Arrow down the incline and gently onto the ferry. The ferryman's boy put chocks before and aft the wheels and collected the fare from Blight.

"Let's get out," said Crispin, and proceeded to do just that. He knelt on one of the benches along the side and, holding onto the rail, leaned back and looked up. Huge clouds drifted overhead, shadowy underneath but towering white above—floating island countries seen from beneath. The boy was on the lookout for Malgrin but could see nothing except an occasional swallow from some nearby barn. A pair of ducks arrowed low over the water and splashed in among the floating yellow leaves from the willows on the bank. Some women with baskets came down the ramp and settled onto the benches. He sauntered over to where Blight was talking to the ferryman.

"It's Longshanks you're looking for?" the ferryman was saying. "It's straight on out of the village, a mile and a half, maybe. You can't miss it. You're going to the sale, I expect."

"The sale," said Blight, evenly, but he raised one eyebrow at Crispin.

"Well, they're selling out, aren't they? You're not the first one to come over this morning looking for Longshanks." He rang the bell; the ferryman's boy cast off and they both fell to cranking the winch that pulled them across the river.

"You heard that?" asked Blight.

"Yes. You don't suppose we've come too late, do you Blight?"

"Well Crispin, there's no use crossing a ferry before you come to it. We're certainly on the right track; so far, so good."

The Wider Water Ferry had not a great deal of wide water to cross but to Crispin the barge seemed to inch its way from shore to shore. Why could they not install an engine in this craft? He walked to the forward end, stood by the chain across the opening and *willed* his way across. But before too long the ferryman's boy was making fast at the opposite shore. The women with the baskets went off first, while Crispin and Blight climbed into the car; the chocks were removed and they drove up the incline directly into the main street of Shanksmare, a small, grey stone village of well-geraniumed window boxes and tiny garden plots overflowing with roses and larkspur.

They were out of Shanksmare before you could clear your throat and bowled along a one-lane country road, hoping they would not meet something coming the other way just over the top of a rise. They did overtake a horse and wagon and had to wait for a wide spot in the road before they could ease past. Meanwhile, another car came up behind them and blew its horn noisily. That frightened the horse and made it restless so that the wagon came very near to scraping the side of the Pierce Arrow as Blight guided it past. The farmer, meanwhile, was offering the car behind them a piece of his mind and trying, to quiet his horse at the same time—operations that seemed designed to cancel each other out.

The sign, when they came to it, read *LONGSHANKS* and, in smaller letters underneath, *Horse Farm.* "I might have known," muttered Blight, "what else?" Beneath that had been tacked another sign: *Estate Sale and Auction TODAY.* Atop the sign a peregrine falcon perched—Malgrin. They pulled into the drive past an ample gatehouse and onto the shoulder to let the man-in-a-hurry go by and then they got out. A quick wing-beat and Malgrin was on Blight's wrist.

"This is the place, I'm sure of that. What took you so long?"

"It takes longer on the ground," Blight reminded the falcon, "to say nothing of the water, eh Crispin?"

"I suppose. Now, what we want, I think, is the old picnic hamper. I've been back and forth over everything several times and even through the barns. The swallows and pigeons cleared out fast enough," chuckled Malgrin. "Ignore all the other hampers or we may be here until the end of the afternoon. The one we want is on a pile of oddments in a stable courtyard, unless they move it. Nobody seems interested in it, yet, but you never know. And we have no time to waste."

"No need to remind us of that," said Blight; and Crispin asked, "Shall we stop back here to open it and see what's inside? If anything."

"That's a fine idea. I'll be watching for you," and Malgrin spread his wings and was gone.

The broad, gravel drive of Longshanks seemed to go on far too long, past fences and more fences but with no horses behind them. The drive curved gently upward, higher and higher until; finally, topping a rise, they came upon the big house and outbuildings standing in the center of a shallow bowl of immaculate green lawns and spacious gardens. The house itself was a great, old pile of a house that looked like the head of a young boy with too many cowlicks: it stuck out in all directions in brick and timbering, gables and slate. Cars and wagons already filled much of the circle before the house and some had even been pulled onto the lawn. Blight found a place for the Pierce Arrow half off the drive but not quite into the flower beds and not too far from the great arch that led into the stable courtyard.

They both got out and went under the arch into the courtyard. Malgrin was right; the place had more hampers than a steamship, all of them with *LONGSHANKS* stenciled on them in burgundy and blue, the colors of the Longshanks Stables. A crowd of farmers, gentlemen farmers, horsemen, horse trainers, and quite a few of the simply curious milled about over the stones of the yard. At one end a platform had been set up for the auctioneer who was joking with some men standing below. A gabble of anticipation rose from the crowd along with wisps of pipe, cigar, and cigarette smoke.

Crispin, like any small boy, could work his way through the crowd with ease and it was not long before he had made a circuit of the entire court and, coming back to Blight, whispered in his ear, "There's no picnic hamper."

"Is there not? Wrong courtyard, for a picnic hamper: or perhaps they've moved it since Malgrin saw it. We ought to be able to find it. Malgrin did say 'the stable courtyard,' if I remember correctly. Maybe there are others. That seems to be the tack room over there. Why don't you take a quick look through there; there may be another exit, while I advance through the stable door yonder. If we don't run into each other back in the works somewhere, then back here in no more than ten minutes. How does that sound?"

"Better than standing here and gnashing our teeth," and the boy was off through the crowd and disappeared through the tack room door.

Inside, the room was large enough to accommodate an extensive racing operation but it was as bare as a cupboard. It smelt of leather and saddle soap and horses but the rows of supports and pegs were empty except for a solitary saddle and bridle probably not up for sale. Some doors into offices stood open and the offices—deserted and empty of contents. The voice of the auctioneer and the calls of bidders in the yard outside only deepened the silence.

Crispin felt as though he should go on tip-toe so as not to disturb the quiet but his sneakers made no noise anyway. At the other end of the room was a door into a passage. He went through the door and down the passage where another open door let in a rectangle of sunshine. Outside was a ribbon of bright sunlight which he crossed glancing both to left and right—nothing; no hamper—and slipped between double doors slightly ajar into a dark barn. He stopped; he could see nothing. Only a narrow shaft of sunlight fell from a high, round window making an ellipse of light on the floor, and beyond that an outline of light around doors at the opposite end.

The boy set off cautiously down the length of the barn. He did not want to stumble over anything or into anything. But his eyes began to grow accustomed to the dark and he stepped out more boldly. He passed the light-shaft which had tiny motes of chaff floating in it, making it look almost solid. He heard the doors behind him shut but paid no attention until he reached the far doors and found them shut fast. He groped for a handle or a latch, found one and tried to raise it but it would not budge. There was no give to it at all.

Wasted time! He turned back toward the original doors but then stopped again. An uneasy feeling began to crawl across his scalp and down his back that he was not alone in the barn. Somehow the darkness seemed to shrink towards him. "Who's here?" he called in a hoarse whisper. But even as he asked he knew. It was the Leopard of Tryce.

"Small boy, do not be afraid . . . yet." The voice was just as Crispin remembered it, grating and metallic, but he could also hear the effort being made to soften it, to make it less threatening. "You are a very intelligent boy; young man, perhaps I should say; far more intelligent than I anticipated. So I have come to make you an offer."

At this point, as though a light were suddenly snapped on in his head, the baleful searchlight eyes of the Leopard were fixed on Crispin so that he could do nothing but look into them. The eyes that he saw looked tired, enormously tired, but terrible with what they knew. They were the eyes of one who craved comforting yet rejected it at any and all levels. Beneath that there was something else that Crispin had no name for. "What offer?" he asked.

"You would like to save the great tree."

"I am *going* to save the great tree if I possibly can."

"Determination: how fitting, and courageous, too. But there is something more important than the great tree . . . . more valuable, too."

"What?"

"The entire forest, with its miles and miles of trees, glades, and meadows, its deer, fox, wolves even, and birds of all kinds, and the fish in its rivers and streams. Wouldn't you like to be the Lord of the Great Forest? Think of it. You have yet to see even half of it. Let your mind play over the length and breadth of it . . . . all yours!"

"For what? What would I have to do?"

"A sensible young man, ready with the correct, the apt question. You will do splendidly! Simply call off this foolish search, forget about the tree and I will give you the entire forest: your own! Lord of the Great Forest."

Crispin was not a greedy boy and he had little idea of wealth, what it could and could not do, what its responsibilities were, and how long it might last. But he loved the forest, what he had seen of it, and he already felt a sort of ownership because he had discovered how to get into and out of it. And so he paused to consider.

He looked again into the eyes of the Leopard and saw again that something else in their depths and he realized what it was. It was death.

"You can't give me the forest; you're dead! And besides, it isn't yours to give, anyway." The boy struggled to control the quaver in his voice and ignore the icy finger pointing at his heart. "Get out of my way," he said between his teeth. "Once again you've made me lose time. I wish you'd go back to your grave or wherever they put you, and stay there!"

"No. No." snarled the Leopard of Tryce. "I will destroy you!"

"Blight says you can't hurt me, only make me lose time and scare me." Gathering himself inside, Crispin marched past the dead Archduke toward the door he had come through.

"You can't get out that way. Those doors are locked,"

"I will find that out when I get there."

"Stop! You are my prisoner."

Crispin did not stop. He was thinking now of the time he had lost and that Blight might be worried and searching for him. He did not run, he walked steadily down the length of the dark barn, opened the door and passed out into the light.

*

Blight looked relieved as Crispin hastened up to him in the big courtyard. "I was trying to decide," He said, "whether to go looking for you or stay here so that we wouldn't miss each other. You look a bit peaked, has something happened?"

"I didn't find the hamper but I found something else."

"Oh. What was that?"

"Can we go back to the car? I can't tell you about it here."

So Crispin and Blight sat in the shade on the running board of the Pierce Arrow and the boy told what had happened. The energy that had supported him through his ordeal was all drained away with the consequence that the whole episode seemed more frightening than when he was actually going through it. His voice broke and Blight put his arm around his shoulder for support.

"By the Lord, Crispin, you've got the guts of a grown man inside you there. Both Greyfell and Malgrin told me that they thought we had a winner in you and I'm sure they're right; have been all along. Catch your breath for a minute or two; you may want to blow your nose. I found a way into the house past the kitchens. I can just feel that hamper waiting for us to find it."

*

They found it in the central courtyard in Lot #76—an attic cleaned out—along with children's toys, among them a wooden soldier on a wooden horse on wooden wheels, and a much larger dappled-grey rocking horse with no tail. There were stacks of books tied up with twine, books that were so dusty Crispin could not make out the titles, a large cardboard carton filled with wooden spools of all different sizes, and a weather vane that was a blue wooden sailor with paddles at the ends of his arms. These were supposed to go around and around in the wind but did not. But they had almost walked past the hamper because it was covered with centuries of dust, and was standing on its end propped against the books. The books had caught Crispin's eye and he had a hand on the hamper to move it out of the way when the feel of the wicker clicked in his brain.

"Blight: look! Here's a big old hamper."

Blight did look, and raised his eyebrows. "Best prospect we've come up with yet. Let's move it out where we can get a *better* look."

They separated it from the rest of the attic leftovers. Much of the dust had been rubbed off the handles bringing it down; it was heavy and unwieldy, but in his excitement, the boy was unaware that his hands were dirty and his face smudged. They set the hamper right side up and took another look. It had no Longshanks stencil on it; that was a good sign. Then they both crouched down and looked at the fastenings in front.

"And look here," said Crispin grimly, "it's the Leopard seal, the Leopard of Tryce himself, just like the one on the scroll! This *must* be what we're looking for. But the seal has been broken."

"I think the best thing to do," said Blight, "would be to find someone to pay for this and get it out of here as quickly as possible. Especially since we have no idea what is inside or how much is left to your quest."

They looked around the deserted courtyard. Doors stood open into various passageways as well as a ground floor window near them that was also open. Crispin thought he detected movement within so he went over to it and leaned in. Inside a small man was sweeping-up. He was somewhat gnarled and brown and had beady eyes looking alert behind rimless glasses.

"Excuse me," said the boy.

The man stopped sweeping and waited.

"We would like to buy this hamper. Could you tell us where we should take it and pay for it?"

"Well, isn't there a table in the entryway hall? With a hawk-faced harpy sitting behind it and with an enormous ledger in front of her? And won't she be tickled to take your money into her greedy clutches? It's through yon door in the corner."

"Thank you, sir," said Crispin, and hurried back to Blight. "It's through that door." They picked up the hamper between them but the young man had to bend over a bit so that the boy was not carrying most of the weight.

"Aye, that's the right door," called the sweeper, "but mind her talons." And they could hear him chuckle to himself.

They sidled through the door indicated into a narrow stone passage which opened, at the other end, into the entrance hall. At the other end of that, the great front door stood wide open showing the gravel drive, the green lawns, and the sunlight beyond. The woman behind the table did not look unpleasant at all—a tweedy-looking woman with hair drawn back into a bun, and half-glasses supported, it was true, by a rather sharp, prominent nose. But her eyes were not unkindly as she looked at them with interest over the tops of her glasses. She was knitting.

They set down their burden and Crispin looked at his hands. He had to remind himself *not* to try wiping his hands on his shorts. "Please, ma'am," Crispin began, "we would like to buy this hamper."

"That small door under the stairs," the woman smiled. "You can wash up in there," and she nodded in the direction of the stairs which rose out of sight in flights and landings above them. They took turns at the small basin, in tepid water, with a sliver of soap. There was a roller-towel of not very absorbent character, and the boy was embarrassed because he seemed to be leaving more dirt on the towel than in the water, but he felt better and cleaner, anyway.

"Now, about this hamper," said the woman, very business-like and sitting ramrod-straight in her chair, "it's from . . . ?"

"Lot #76," said Crispin, his heart beating more and more rapidly as he realized that he had no money at all and no idea what the old hamper might cost.

"Right: from the west attic," and she wiffled through the pages of the ledger until . . . "Here we are." She paused. "That's strange." She looked at Crispin, then up at Blight; "It says 'thirty pieces of silver.'"

"An interesting price: what denomination?" asked Blight.

"It doesn't say. The handwriting is different, too, from everything else on the page. I had better ask."

While the woman was getting up from the table and gathering the ledger under her arm, Crispin looked up to Blight in great concern at this new delay. He smiled encouragement and the boy turned back to the table. The woman opened one half of a large double door behind her and went through, leaving the door open. He was looking into a great hall with windows high up and streams of sunlight slanting down making boxes of light and shadow on the floor. The woman made her way through these towards two figures at the other end of the hall. One was a girl seated in a wheel-chair with a blanket over her lap; the other a stocky man just going grey at the temples. The woman showed the ledger to this man and gestured with her head toward the open door. The girl turned and looked down the hall in Crispin's direction.

"Boy." Her voice carried clearly down the full length of the great room. "You there: boy! Come here." He hesitated. "Please." (Clearly an afterthought.) He could feel Blight's hand in his back, gently pushing him forward. He walked the length of the hall (it was as big as a church) being alternately blinded by sunlight and submerged in shadow. As he drew nearer he could see that the girl was two or three years older than he, pale, with pale red hair cut short and eyes that were lively but unsmiling and, again, pale. He stopped at a respectful distance.

"You want to buy that old hamper, do you, boy?"

"Yes, miss."

"Hmmmmmm." She laid a finger across her chin and touched her lower lip. "Do you think we should let him have it, Dads?"

"It's your call, sweetheart," said the man standing behind her. Crispin barely glanced at the man, who was moderately tall, round-faced, and looked as though he spent most of his time out of doors.

"What is your name?" the girl asked.

"Crispin . . . Crispin Agincroft."

"Hmmmmmm. Have you a middle name?"

"Actually, I have two: Timothy and Eilif." He looked at her steadily; he had been taught not to be afraid to look people in the eyes. "What's your name?" he asked.

"Sarah Falkrest. I have no middle name. I used to have but I didn't like it so I'm considering other possibilities. Where are you from, Crispin Timothy Eilif Agincroft? Not from around here, I think. The name is unfamiliar. Do you recognize it, Dads?"

"I believe I may have heard it at one time or another, but it's not a . . . racing name; perhaps somewhere in the next county over."

The man had pronounced the word *racing* with some hesitation, as though embarrassed by it, and Sarah, looking up at her father, said, "Our racing days seem to be pretty well over, anyway; mine . . . permanently. This, by the way, is my father, Colonel Falkrest. He owns this whole operation. Barely. Don't you Dads." She took hold of his arm and rubbed her cheek against his sleeve.

"I'm pleased to meet you, sir," and Crispin and Colonel Falkrest shook hands.

"Well?" and Sarah turned back to the boy.

"Blight and I came over this morning on the Wider Water Ferry. Blight lives at Priorfields; I live on the *other* side of the forest." He turned to see what had become of Blight and saw that he was standing just inside the double doors at the other end of the hall.

"Blight is that young man with the cropped beard down there?"

"Yes, that's right."

"Hmmmmmm." Again the girl laid her finger across her chin onto her lower lip. "And why do you want to buy the hamper?"

Deep within, Crispin had felt this question approaching ever since there was the difficulty about the price. He straightened his back (which didn't need it), took a deep breath, and looked Sarah squarely in the eyes. "I am on a quest, and I think the hamper is part of it. Or at least I hope so."

For the first time the girl's eyes sparkled. "*You're* on a quest, and I'm a damsel in distress," and she banged on the arms of her wheelchair and laughed. "It's all right about the price, Mrs. Presskit; I wrote it in the ledger and I'll take care of it. You did exactly the right thing by coming to ask. Thank you." Mrs. Presskit retired down the length of the hall, taking the ledger with her.

During this maneuver Crispin took out his big watch and clicked it open. He saw that it was almost one-thirty and felt a tightening of panic around his scalp and in the pit of his stomach. He glanced up and saw that Sarah was watching him with interest. "What can you tell me about your quest?" she asked.

He snapped the watch shut, stuffed it back into his pocket and said, "That it ends tonight at sundown and that if I haven't achieved it by then I never will."

"And that you would like to take the hamper and leave as quickly as possible, is that right?"

"Yes. I'm sorry, but it is."

"As you may have noticed, the seal on the hamper is broken. I did that myself. I opened it and know what is inside. That is why I put that price on it. You will understand when you open it, I think. I took nothing out. Take the hamper as my gift, my share in your quest. Just promise that if you achieve it you will return and tell me about it. You promise?" They shook hands and she continued, "I don't see any young people at all . . . and Dads is struggling to hang onto the house and land. We lost mother just before I was stricken—double jeopardy," she said, with grim irony, "or triple, if you throw in the horses. Now that I can no longer ride myself, I am learning to . . . appreciate . . . other things." Her voice faltered momentarily but she recovered. "I would be very grateful to know that *some*thing turned out for the best."

Crispin swallowed hard. "I will come back and tell you all about it: whether I achieve it or not. Good bye and thank you for the hamper; thank you very much." He turned and started back down the hall, but paused and called over his shoulder, "And for understanding!"

SIXTEEN

THE HAMPER AND THE QUEST

"We lead lives crowded with incident; unpredictable at best; unconscionable at worst." Blight was lying on his back under a tree with his arms crossed behind his head. He was feeling reflective and philosophical; talking to Malgrin perched above him. Malgrin, it must be admitted, was paying Blight no heed. He was lost in his own reflections. With his head sunk between his shoulders, and his eyes narrowed to slits, the crowded incidents he pondered had to do with tender, furry bellies and pink feet. Crispin lay fast asleep in the shade of the same tree, the big watch lying open and unregarded near his ear. Eating lunch had done it. He had been wide awake until his stomach was filled with sandwiches, milk still cool from the thermos, and a piece of chocolate cake almost twice the size his mother would have cut for him.

Blight had pulled the Pierce Arrow close up to the deserted gate house where it too was in the shade. They had taken the hamper carefully down from the roof of the car where it had been strapped; they brought it to the shade of a great copper beech tree and opened it, the seal having already been broken by Sarah. As they were doing this they tried to fill Malgrin in on the events of the preceding few hours. Sometimes Crispin talked in rambling, unpunctuated sentences, distracted as he was by anticipation of what the hamper might hold. Sometimes Blight talked in short sentences meant to bridge gaps left by the boy. At one point they both talked at once and then they both fell silent at the same time. Through all of this the falcon was remarkably patient, keeping his eye fixed on the hamper.

Crispin opened it. It was not an ordinary commercial picnic hamper with straps to hold plates and cups and saucers, but simply a hamper that may have been used to pack foodstuffs wanted on a journey or voyage. The boy lifted out a large piece of folded linen and laid it carefully aside. Beneath the linen were two pieces of leather that had been worked to the softness of silk. One was carefully folded around a large silver plate and the other had been sewn into an ingenious envelope containing a silver goblet to match the plate. The goblet made Crispin think of what the Holy Grail might have looked like.

These two pieces had been worked down into a nest of what at first appeared to be cobblestones.

The boy picked one up and passed it to his companion; "They can't be stones, can they? They're too light."

"You know, I think they're loaves of bread thoroughly dried out and preserved for who knows how long?"

Dust had filtered through the wicker and the boy took a deep breath and blew on a loaf before putting it to his nose. "Oh. Sorry . . . wrong direction." Blight was putting on an act of coughing and choking. "They don't smell like bread. They don't smell like anything. But you must be right, but they're smaller than the loaves I'm used to. They look about like mother's dinner rolls."

He continued to take out the little loaves and stack them carefully in the grass. Beneath them, in the bottom of the hamper, was a row of earthenware bottles alternately laid in opposite directions. These too were dust-covered except one that Sarah had obviously lifted out, cleaned off, and then replaced. Crispin lifted the same bottle out now and set it in the grass with the loaves.

"It's wine, isn't it? Sarah told me I would understand about the price when I saw what was inside. Thirty pieces of silver." He looked at Blight: "The price of Him who was priced."

"What does it say on the bottle?"

"I don't know; I can't read it."

Blight picked up the bottle gently and looked at the incised name. "*Sang de Sorciere Noir*," he read: "Blood of the Black Witch. That's a relief; that's one less worry we have to worry about."

"You mean there *isn't* any Black Witch? Not at all?"

"I think it's a safe bet. Are you disappointed?

"Not at all."

And Malgrin from his perch said, "I have felt from the very beginning that there was no Black Witch but I hesitated to say so, probably lest I be proved wrong. However, nowhere in my family lore or in the lore of the forest, as it has been passed on to me by Greyfell, nowhere have I heard of a black witch, only that rather ineffectual nasty that wound up in Greyfell's pot. Now, would one of you please explain the mystery about the price of the hamper?"

Blight took the falcon on his wrist and talked to him in a low voice while Crispin continued to feel gently under the bottles for a piece of parchment.

"Ahhhhh, the One who is to come," said the falcon softly as light dawned. And then, "Crispin, I think what you are looking for maybe on the inside of the cover."

In opening the hamper the boy had not even glanced at the cover but simply put it over on its leather hinges so that it hung down in back, facing away from the boy squatting in front of it. Now he stood up and looked over.

There it was, held tightly to the lip of the hamper-lid by strong threads that had been carefully worked through the wicker and tied, a long, narrow scroll, practically invisible to anyone in a hurry and not looking for it.

Crispin complimented the falcon, "Oh, eyes that are so much sharper than mine, thank you. I never saw it at all, although it was the one thing I was looking for."

"Sometimes you can see things better if you are *not* looking for them," said Malgrin, generously. "Besides, it was probably obscured by your left hand and arm as you pushed back the lid."

Crispin hauled out his grandfather's watch and opened the pen knife that hung at the other end of the chain. With this he carefully slit through the heavy threads until the scroll was freed. He blew the dust off, but this time in the *right* direction. The parchment had been rolled up so tightly and for so long that it resisted the boy's careful efforts to unroll it.

"Let me hold this end," said Blight, putting a hand down over the scroll. "Now you can unroll the other end and hold that with your right. Ah! Now you're in business."

The boy looked carefully at the open scroll. "It's different handwriting," he said. "This is much easier to read; what can *that* mean? But it's signed TRYCE. That seems to be the same hand as the first."

"Perhaps this was done by a secretary or a scribe; it is certainly much easier to read. What have we got this time?" Blight had stretched himself out in the grass; he propped himself on his elbows next to Crispin.

"I am waiting with breath abated," rasped the falcon from his branch, "and I sense an assemblage of crows gathering somewhere in the wings (a theatrical metaphor, I believe); I may have to desert my post shortly. It's only your presence, I suspect, that holds them at bay."

The boy knit his brows, cleared his throat, and began to read aloud:

> "The first broom shall be destroyed by which?
> By water, earth; by air or fire?
> The second broomstick thou shalt find
> At rest in what destroyed the first.
> Retrieve what hangs between the ears
> Of the legendary boar;
> To the landlord take the shard,
> He will supply the final shred.
> Tick tock, mind the clock,
> The sand in the glass runs away;
> Turn tide; sun hide
> And night replace seventh day."

"Oh rats! Rats! Ten thousand rats!" Crispin let go of his end of the scroll and it rolled up with a snap. "I was hoping this would be the last clue. How many more can there be? And how many more do we have time for?"

"Now my young friend, if I recommend patience you will probably pop me one on the end of the nose, so let me recommend realism instead. Only one bridge, only one ferry can be crossed at a time. If you knew how many bridges you had to cross you might give up too early. As it is, you can only go forward with hope. And help from your friends."

During this speech Crispin had risen to his feet and stood listening to Blight's words with his fists clenched, his teeth grit, and thunderclouds forming about his brow. "But I *want* to save the great tree," he said through clenched teeth, "and I don't even know whether it can be done or not. Maybe it's just a joke, or a hoax, and the Leopard is just leading me on and laughing up his sleeve."

"Well, about that: he made you an offer, such as it was; would he have done that if he were not worried? Perhaps you are closer than you think."

"I suppose that's a possibility. I wonder if it could be true."

"Sour is the taste of disappointment," Malgrin was quoting a family axiom, "Don't eat it unless you have to."

The boy's jaw relaxed a little, then his fists unclenched and he put his hands into his pockets and the storm clouds cleared off. "Now suppose you read us the scroll again," suggested his companion cheerfully. Crispin read it again clearly, carefully, distinctly.

"With regard to the verse, I have always felt that *inevitability* was one of the characteristics of good poetry, that *these* words simply had to be put in *this* order and would be unsuccessful in any other. This is clearly not the case with these words; in fact, almost any *other* order would seem preferable. Except that last bit, I rather like that. It is reminiscent of 'Hickory Dickory Dock' or 'Jack Sprat.'"

The boy cocked his head and looked directly at Blight. Then, with a perfectly straight face, he said, "Don't be pompous, it is unbecoming in small boys." But he could not keep the tell-tale sparkle out of his eyes and so his companion asked, "Does your mother know my mother? I think they must have put their heads together. That is exactly what mine would have said. And now, I think we deserve lunch."

They had wrapped themselves in the shadow of the tree and ate sandwiches ("Don't eat the peanut butter and jelly, I need those.") and drank milk from thermos cups, and both had a large slice of chocolate cake. Hardly had they finished lunch when the boy fell asleep as though he had been clubbed, his right hand under his cheek and his left grasping the open watch before his closed eyes, the chain and pen knife curling away into the mossy grass. Deep, deep into sleep he dropped, his hand relaxed on the watch, his breathing became regular. Then, in the depths, shadows gathered and searchlight eyes sought for him in the dark.

*

"How long are you going to let him sleep?" Malgrin asked, grasping and re-grasping his branch impatiently.

"Ten . . . fifteen minutes at the most."

"Time and tide . . . ."

"I think we can spare fifteen, but no more. The boy has had a long day already and we have no idea what else lies in store for him. Or for us," Blight added. Then he picked up what was left of the lunch, collected the wax papers and thermos cups and bottle, plus the basket, and stowed everything into the trunk of the car. He repacked the big hamper carefully, leaving out the scroll which they would need to consult. The hamper just fit into the trunk next to the picnic basket. That accomplished, he stretched himself out under the tree and began to spin out the philosophy of his young life as he had experienced it thus far. Meanwhile Crispin slept.

*

"Time . . . what time is it? You've let me sleep!" The boy was on his hands and knees staring down at the big timepiece, trying to make sense out of what it said without realizing that he was looking at it upside down.

Blight consulted his own watch. "Twelve minutes with some seconds to spare."

"Why did you let me sleep? Come on, let's go!"

"Because I thought you needed some sleep, to answer your question. Everything is picked up and packed up. We can leave immediately."

The boy walked briskly to the car, not forgetting to put the watch and chain back in his pocket. He opened the door, climbed in, and shut the door. The young man looked at the falcon and said, "Don't fly away quite yet." He got in behind the wheel, put the key in the ignition and then asked, "Which way?"

"Oh: Which way, what do you think?"

"You're the boss of this expedition. What do *you* think?"

Crispin sat for a minute, then, "The first scroll said (I think it was the last direction), oh, how did it go? . . . . 'From this, a new direction take.' So I don't think we should go back across the ferry. Should we look at the map?"

Blight considered. "The other way out of Shanksmare will take us along the southern edge of the forest, on *this* side of the river. That means if we are going to get back in time we may have to go through Tryceholdings. There is no road through the forest except the one you took last night and one to the wharf opposite Shipman's Brink. And no bridges across the river, with or without green bay leaves."

"Then we have no choice, do we?"

"Not if we're to take a new direction." Blight stuck his head out the window and called to the falcon, "West out of Shanksmare."

SEVENTEEN

THE LEGENDARY BOAR AT BAY

West out of Shanksmare the road wound and dipped, sometimes following the river closely, sometimes making wild swings around fields and farms or plunging through tiny villages like Cutting Edge or Woodbore, and once creeping through the large town known as Shipman's Brink. Never were they out of sight of the river for very long and consequently never out of sight of the forest. Close along the river bank Crispin could scent the pine and juniper and feel (he thought) the forest breathing. Close across the river it stood like a towering green curtain waiting to go up and reveal the mysteries behind it. The boy held his breath.

"Blight, suppose the legendary boar lives in the forest. How will we ever find it in time?"

"I suppose there are still wild boar in the forest, quite a few by this time since nobody has hunted them for hundreds of years; as well as wolves and bears. Anyway, the directions we have to go on indicate *this* side of the river. But they could be deliberately misleading." The boy's eyes had been straining back and forth over the countryside, looking for any indication of the presence of a boar. At every farmhouse and cottage they passed he looked for a pigpen and wondered what it might contain.

Blight was consoling. "So far everything has been very straightforward, once we figured it out. We did find the hamper and the Blood of the Black Witch inside. All we can do is go forward, making what speed we can on this snake's back."

Hardly had he said that when the road straightened out and ran as straight as a spear shaft for almost two miles. It was a relief, for a change, to be able to see what was coming a long way off.

What they saw was a man standing by the edge of the road. He was wearing riding boots and a dark green hunting coat and was stroking the nose of a long-legged, red horse that could have been one of Longshanks' finest.

"Stop! Blight stop!" and Crispin put a hand on Blight's arm.

But Blight had already begun to slow down and pump the brakes. They had both noticed that, in place of a saddle blanket on the horse, there was a leopard skin.

Experienced driver that he was, Blight brought the car to a standstill just next to the horseman. The boy put one knee on the seat and leaned out the open window.

"Good afternoon," he said. "This may sound strange but we're trying to find a legendary boar."

"Yes, of course." The man looked thoughtfully at Crispin, who felt, beneath his piercing gaze, that his entire young history was being absorbed and understood in a matter of seconds. He looked at Blight not at all. "Just a little over a mile further along and then to your right down the lane."

The boy raised his eyebrows in surprise and looked pleased, but the man continued to look intently into and almost through him. He was a well set-up man of forty or forty-five, slightly taller than Blight and not yet beginning to settle or spread. Dark hair with an odd streak of white over his right eye, a complexion brown from the out-of-doors, and that piercing gaze that asked everything and knew everything at one and the same time, these completed the picture.

"Thank you, sir." The man nodded. Crispin drew in his head and sat down again as the automobile rolled forward. Then he turned again and knelt on the seat looking out of the rear window. The man had mounted his horse and, with practically no preparation at all, they leapt the hedge across the road and disappeared from sight. The boy turned once more and sat down next to Blight.

"He looks like Malgrin," he said.

"His horse certainly took off like a great bird."

"Did you see that!" exclaimed the boy.

"Yes: in the rear view mirror; remarkable! I don't think I've ever seen anything quite like it."

"I don't understand it. He almost seemed to be expecting me. And eyes! I'll bet he could read the label in the back of my shirt."

They sped on for a mile and Blight slowed down, a mile, then a quarter, and there was a stone post at the corner of a lane to the right. The stone post had a mail box built into its middle but there was no name.

"Must be it," said Blight, turning right. The lane was well-traveled; it rose slightly through a grove of gnarled oak, like a portion of the forest spilled over onto this side of the river. The lane ended in the cobbled yard of a low stone building that looked like a series of afterthoughts or second guesses. Yet, in spite of its low eaves and abundant chimneys, there was something austere about it, perhaps because its windows, spacious enough, rose to pointed arches, giving it a vaguely monastic character.

They rolled to a stop before what was evidently the main door and over which hung a signboard. The lettering had weathered almost beyond recognition but there could be no mistaking what it said: *The Legendary Boar.*

No other cars or trucks, nor horses either, stood in the yard. No one leaned out of windows or doorways to see who had driven in. Not even a curtain fluttered. Only Malgrin dropped from above onto the signboard and stood with his head between his legs, trying to make it out upside down.

"It says, 'The Legendary Boar," said Crispin, coming to his aid.

Blight said, "This must be it. The right place."

"But, what about the ears? 'Between the ears of the legendary boar'"

"Let's go inside."

He had to duck his head going through the door which groaned heavily on its hinges as he pushed it open and stepped through. The boy followed him in. They stood on the stone floor of a snug taproom with a few wooden benches, stools, and small tables pushed randomly about, a large, low hearth in which glowed the remains of a small fire (not quite enough to take the chill off), and a narrow bar at the back of the room opposite the door. This likewise served the room beyond, which looked larger and brighter. A passage led from one room to the other. There was no one about.

"A deserted inn," Crispin whispered, looking warily behind the door.

Blight walked up to the bar and was just about to rap on it with his knuckles when a low door opened inside the bar and a large figure climbed agilely into the small space. Blight's jaw dropped and Crispin gasped.

"I thought I would get here ahead of you," said the man from the roadside, "but I gather you are in a great hurry." He had removed his green coat and was wearing a collarless blue and white stripped shirt with the sleeves turned back. "What can I do for you?" he asked, and automatically picked up a pint glass and began polishing it with a dish towel.

"The . . . the legendary . . . boar?" Crispin could barely get the words out; he was so choked with surprise.

"Ah yes, of course." Once again his eyes looked deep into the boy's own eyes: "in the next room here. Just follow along that passage." He indicated the one at the opposite end of the bar, behind the taps and, while the boy and his companion walked through, let himself out through the hinged bar in back.

"Here he is," he said, as they emerged into the room, and he extended his arm toward a cavernous great fireplace with inglenooks on both sides. Dimly, in the depths, up over the hearthstone, Crispin and Blight saw, more clearly as they advanced toward it, the head of a gigantic, stuffed boar gazing ferociously at them with tusks bared.

"Holy Casmittima," breathed the boy.

And Blight said, "I have *never* seen anything like it. Do you mind if we examine it closely?" He turned to the host to find him still watching Crispin with his hawk-like eyes.

"Not in the least. I would be very interested if you did. It has been here almost as long as the building. Long, long before I was born. It holds up remarkably well."

"Give me a leg up, Blight, please?" the boy asked. He put his foot into the cup made by Blight's hands, rested a hand upon his shoulder and then on the top of his head as he came level with the staring little eyes of the boar. He could now see that they were made of glass, and felt better about that.

"A bit cobwebby, I'm afraid," remarked their host, but it was a statement, not an apology.

"Between the ears of the legendary boar," the boy muttered half to himself, as he clutched Blight's curly hair and raised his left hand past the snout and tusks and eyes and felt carefully through the bristly hair around the ears and as far down the back as he could reach.

"Nothing."

"Try again," said Blight, adjusting his position carefully.

The boy tried again, not knowing exactly what it might be he was looking for.

"No, nothing."

The young man carefully lowered Crispin to the floor, hearing, all too clearly, the disappointment in his voice.

"You are looking for something. Can I be of any help? Perhaps a flashlight would help? I can get one quite easily." The man had seated himself in one of the inglenooks where his face was completely in shadows and the light caught only the sheen on his boots.

"No. There's no point. There's nothing there." The boy's disappointment was turning to bitterness.

"We are looking for something that is supposed to be between the ears of 'the legendary boar.' Do you know if anyone has ever removed anything from this head?"

"No: never. I would have known. And the family has kept careful records over the years. I have been through them all very thoroughly—it's part of my responsibility—there is no record of *any* removals." The last bit he said very distinctly, with such emphasis, that it made Blight stare into the shadows of the nook.

"Who *are* you anyway? My name is Blight," and he held out his hand so that the man had to stand up, back into the light.

"I'm sorry. I should have told you at once. Riverford's my name, Frederick Riverford. But most people call me Fritz." They shook hands cordially

"And this is . . ." Blight turned to where the boy had crawled into the opposite nook. There he sat cross-legged, with his head in his hands, struggling with his bitter frustration.

"Yes, I know. Crispin Agincroft."

"But how on earth do you know that?" the boy asked, hoarsely clearing away the lump in his throat and looking up with great surprise.

"Follow me and I'll show you."

He led the way back into the bar and through the low door ("Mind your heads!") down a stone stairway into an arched cellar, past great hogsheads and casks and shelves of dusty bottles, then outside through a narrow door cut into a much larger one. They stood on a stone platform for loading and unloading. To their left was an arch that led into the cobbled yard, but they went down stone steps on their right and stood at the river's edge. They were standing on a broad stone ramp that sloped down from the yard to the water's edge, into the water three or four feet below the surface and just out again on the opposite side. The swift water flashed and quarreled over it in a gurgling roar and then flowed on deeply as before. A family of chimney swifts dipped over the water, catching drinks, but they disappeared in a flash as Malgrin dropped onto a branch.

Blight exclaimed, "The ford! Of course, 'river ford.' How dumb! And he slapped his forehead. "I heard there was one but I could never find it in a single day. It's the rear door of the forest. Who *are* you, anyway?"

"My post is that of Guardian of the Ford, after which we took our name. That's how I knew the boy's name; news in the forest travels swifter than swifts."

Riverford and Blight fell into an animated conversation but Crispin sat down on the edge of the ramp, picked up a pebble and tossed it into the water, and then another. Glancing up he saw Malgrin perched on a leafless branch regarding him fixedly.

"Come bird," the boy said without any spirit, and the falcon flitted to his shoulder.

"Tell me," rasped Malgrin.

"Between the ears of the legendary boar there is exactly nothing. Not anything." Then he said it to himself again, "Between the ears . . . between . . . What could that possibly mean? . . . the ears . . . between the . . ." Somewhere something shifted in his imagination. " . . . the ears . . . between . . ."

Then Malgrin whispered into his ear, "Between the ears."

But he had already understood.

"Blight: quick! I know where it is. Mr. Riverford, sir, we have to go back. Hurry! I know where it is!"

He darted up the stairs, across the platform and disappeared the way they had come out, with the bird clinging to his shoulder and flapping its wings to maintain balance. The other two followed just as quickly.

Between them they hoisted the boy up next to the legendary boar. The falcon had taken refuge in a pair of antlers elsewhere in the room, loathing to be enclosed but not wanting to miss a thing, not any more. Crispin took a deep breath and reached in through the gaping maw and deadly tusks of the boar and felt upward. Way in past his elbow he had to reach. He found what he was searching for, gave a determined yank, and carefully extracted his arm. In his hand was a small circle of folded parchment with a heavy thread running through it.

They lowered the boy to the floor and followed him to a western window. The sun was still high enough that it made only a narrow rectangle on the floor. Blight's eyes sparkled and Frederick Riverford looked remarkably pleased.

Crispin unfolded the parchment, his fingers trembling; it said, *This is the one. Open.*

"Those are my instructions," said their host. "I will be happy to oblige."

While he disappeared behind the counter of the bar, the boy recited, "To the landlord take the shard, / He will supply the final shred."

The landlord returned with a small iron casket of impregnable design and set it down on a table and put an iron key down next to it. Then he stepped back and looked expectantly at Crispin who then sat down before the casket, took the key and fitted it into the lock. He turned it smoothly (it had apparently been kept well-oiled) and lifted the cover. There was a single slip of parchment; a single line had been scrawled across it. He picked it up and read aloud: *In the fire across the Stone of Harklinden.* Beneath that, just the initial **T** and a splash of wax the color of dried blood with the leopard seal pressed into it.

"Where or what is Harklinden?" Crispin looked up at Blight.

"That must be the Abbey; it was dedicated to Our Lady of Harklinden. But what the Stone of Harklinden is, I have no idea," and Blight looked at Frederick Riverford.

"Nor have I," he said. "I have come across nothing in my travels through the Forest that would qualify." All three turned to Malgrin.

"No. I'm sorry. Could it be inside the Abbey building?"

But the boy interrupted, "I've heard that name before I read this, I'm sure of it." He put both pieces of parchment down on the table next to the casket and noticed that there was something else inside. A large, gold signet ring had lain concealed under the parchment. He held it up and a gold chain, which ran through the ring, dripped down and swung back and forth. "What's this?"

"That, I believe, is the Ring of Harklinden," Frederick Riverford looked at it carefully. "Yes, it has the seal of the Abbey on it. The ring belongs to you; at least you have achieved that." The Guardian of the Ford took the ring and placed the chain over the boy's head. "Someday your finger will grow into the ring and then you can discard the chain."

"Thank you," said the boy somewhat doubtfully, "but what does it all mean? Harklinden, where do I know that name from?"

"You will discover that if you are the one to achieve the quest. And everything points in your direction."

"You can give me no help?"

"Even if I could, I couldn't. But, as it turns out, I have criss-crossed the forest and my father before me and *his* father before him and so on back through my family. We never found what it might be."

But Crispin was no longer listening. He stuck a finger through the ring and turned it idly, paying no attention. Where had he heard that name before? Where? When? No, he hadn't *heard* it, but he had *seen* it. Where? Why did he keep thinking of his own front door? Because . . . under the large doormat outside there was a stone slab even larger than the mat. But under the mat, there it was! The single word carved into the stone in capital letters: *HARKLINDEN.*

"It's at my own front door," he said, then reached into his pocket and fished out the other directions: "'The second broomstick thou shalt find / At rest in what destroyed the first.' That's fire. Greyfell chopped it up and threw it in his fire and it exploded: 'In the fire across the Stone of Harklinden.' That could mean that the second broom has also been burnt up. But then we couldn't find it. What is across the stone? . . . my front door! And . . . ?"

He looked at Blight with shining eyes. "It's the hearth boom in the fireplace in our little library just inside the front door. It's "at rest" there. I've seen it myself. O Blight that's it! I'm sure of it!" And he jumped up and gave Blight a big hug around his waist and pumped the hand of Guardian Fritz. Then he looked up at Malgrin and said, "Haven't you seen it, sometime when the mat was pulled aside?"

"No, not I:" He flew to Blight's shoulder. The boy was much too excited to afford a safe perch and he wanted to get back outside in the worst way.

They streamed back through the snug taproom and outside to the waiting automobile. Malgrin said, "I will meet you at the great tree," and he took off, circling up and up and disappearing over the treetops of the forest.

"If you don't mind," said Fritz Riverford, "I will saddle my horse and meet you at the tree myself. I think Vortex can get me there before sundown."

Crispin said, "I hope *we* can get there before sundown." He was pushing Blight toward the car with both hands but paused long enough to shake hands with the innkeeper of *The Legendary Boar* and then Blight shook hands as well while the boy climbed into the car and beeped the horn impatiently.

"All right, all right," said Blight good-naturedly, sliding behind the wheel. "We're on our way."

And Frederick Riverford was already striding toward the stable.

EIGHTEEN

THROUGH TRYCEHOLDINGS

"Who *was* that?"

"Frederick Riverford?"

"Yes."

They had come out of the lane onto the narrow county road. But they had to slow down almost immediately as they caught up to a hay wagon drawn by a team of horses. Once again Crispin was reminded of the wagons that pass on the road by his house. Now he had no patience for farm wagons and leaned out the window to see whether they could squeeze past. It looked hopeless. He pulled in his head and shoulders and turned back to Blight.

"The Guardian of the Ford."

"Yes, yes. I heard him say that, but then I stopped listening."

"He is the result of the bend sinister in the Tryce family tree."

"The bend sinister? I don't understand."

"You remember my telling you that long ago, long, *long* ago, there had been vague rumors of an illegitimate son of the Archduke? A half-brother therefore of Blaise and Axel?"

"Yes, of course I remember." The boy's impatience with the hay wagon had not diminished.

"Someone systematically scotched the rumors, probably the Archduke himself, until there wasn't even a whisper. Nevertheless—"

"They had been true," interrupted Crispin, who stuck his head back out the window and was about to shout "Hey!" to the farmer driving the load, thought better of it, drew in his head again and apologized to Blight for interrupting.

But the next moment he burst out, "Holy Casmittima, will this wagon *never* turn off?"

Blight was silent. They drove in silence for another minute. Then the wagon turned into a farmyard and the Pierce Arrow sped up, again living up to its name.

Still they drove in silence.

"Please tell me about the bend sinister." The boy, embarrassed and much chastened, looked up at his companion.

"It is the sign in heraldry that a family line is illegitimate, a dark band across the field. The Archduke sequestered the mother and the son, giving them the first little stone cottage by the ford and enough acres to keep them healthy. He may have confessed to the Abbot of Harklinden because the Abbot made the boy Guardian of the Ford. If that is true, the secret of the boy's origin died with the Abbot but lived in the memory of mother and son and gradually found its way into the family records. After naming the boy Frederick, mother and son took the name Riverford. Ever since, the family has lived by the ford, guarding it from poachers and other predators and interlopers, and never, repeat NEVER, making a claim on the Tryce estate. All the various Fredericks grew up in the forest, learning all of its lingoes, its paths and by-paths, everything."

"But you never ran into each other?"

"No, I was never expecting to run into anyone, which probably made me careless. And then, after my encounter with the Leopard of Tryce, I stuck pretty much to the high paths and in broad daylight. I never managed to get all the way through the forest to the other edge. Who knows? If I had gone looking for the ford I may have found it. Most probably I would."

"Of course you would. You could find anything in the forest, I'll bet. How far are we from Tryceholdings?"

"About four miles: I've been counting the milestones."

"Are there milestones? I never noticed."

"You have other things on your mind. The next one should be along any minute. I suppose there's a gas station somewhere in Tryceholdings. I would hate to run out of gas at the last minute. Yes, here it comes now."

As they sailed over the top of a small rise, the boy saw a large block of granite embedded in the bank with a large 4 carved deep into it.

"Here comes 3," he exclaimed a little later as they approached the next. Then they caught up with another automobile which they could not pass because there was one coming in the opposite direction, and then another one and then they just got by in time in a straight stretch but it did not make any difference because they entered Tryceholdings over the bridge and through the South Gate and slowed to a crawl.

Rather than a station, they found a gas pump attended by a stringy youngster. The pump had been let into a brick wall and Blight had to get two wheels up onto the sidewalk before the hose would reach. Horns blew in the narrow street, pedestrians along the sidewalk complained to the youngster, who kept up a steady stream of disrespectful banter to all and sundry, whether they were leaning out of car windows shouting or ducking under or stepping over the hose. Blight paid for the gas and tipped the youngster a fat coin. He promptly started calling Blight "Captain" and ran into the street, whistling through his teeth and giving lip back to angry drivers; stopping traffic, so "the Captain" could get the car off the sidewalk.

All streets worked their way through the town by way of the High Market, at the upper end of which was the great pile that had been the stronghold of the Archdukes, Tryceholdings Guard. It was now the Town Hall and County Court House. All traffic flowed into the High Market, up one side and down the other, braking and shifting to avoid people circulating through the stalls of the market, beeping and blowing horns behind automobiles that had stopped so that drivers could chat with neighbors or hawkers-of-goods, the whole scene a turmoil of live chickens upside down with their legs tied together, armloads of rhubarb and cabbages and beets, children wailing and digging in their heels, parents dragging them along to the next booth, cattle lowing, a pig squealing, buyers haggling with sellers, a gentleman or two, oblivious of all, leaning over the second-hand book stall, the whirr and chug of motors, the smell of exhaust and horse droppings, all of it mostly good-natured and exasperating.

It took them a good fifteen minutes to circumnavigate the market. As they approached the top, Crispin leaned out and looked up at the forbidding gatehouse. Standing atop it was a great stone coat of arms, supported on either side by a leopard rampant. He wondered which of them was *his* leopard and whether he would meet her again, later.

Then they started down the other side of High Market and now the boy wished that youngster from the gas pump was still whistling and shouting and making way for them. Crispin had never heard anything quite like him and thought he must have the fastest lip in the West.

More than halfway down the market a street ran off to the right underneath an arch above which rose an ugly-looking guard tower. Compared to the market, the street seemed empty and in almost no time they drove out through the North Gate, down the steep slope that led up to it.

High above the town, on the very brink of the gate house tower of Tryceholdings Guard, one of the leopards blinked her eyes and disappeared, although it was impossible to tell that she was gone.

NINETEEN

DESERTED

"There it is," Crispin shouted excitedly as they came over the final rise and saw, first the chimneys, the roof and the tower, and then the grey house itself and the outbuildings, all sitting secure and comfortable by the side of the road. "The tower is next to my own room." He had to pull his head in the window and turn to Blight to tell him this.

"I like it already," Blight replied, taking his foot off the accelerator and beginning to brake. The boy directed him to "just pull in through the arch."

But when they got there, the great, blue wooden gates into the courtyard were shut up tight. That was very strange; why was this? The boy could never recall having seen the gates closed before. "Hang on," he said, "I'll open them."

He opened the car door and jumped down off the running board, ran to the gates, lifted the big latch-handle and pushed. The gates did not budge. "They must be barred from inside," he shouted to Blight. Next he tried the latch on the wicket-gate, but that was held tight by the same bar that secured the big gates. Crispin stepped back into the road and looked up: At the top of the high wall, at one side of the arch, hung a large bell in a stone bell house. A bell-rope for travelers hung down on the outside next to the gate. Apparently this rope had been meant for adults, or people on horseback; it ended in a large knot too high for the boy to reach. He had to jump up as high as he could and grab the knot. He did that now, grasped the knot and gave the rope a mighty pull as he dropped back into the road. The bell rang once, an iron note to announce the homecoming, a note that rang and reechoed through the invisible courtyard. But the rope had rotted and never been replaced, and it dropped into the road beside Crispin, who still held the other end of it in his hand.

There was no response from inside.

Perplexed, the boy looked at Blight, who had pulled off on the other side of the road and gotten out. "Nobody home?" he suggested lightly.

"There must be. Wait here, the tower gate *has* no lock." He ran along the wall, turned the corner, and went around behind a long shed that made the fourth wall of the court. Near the end of the house where the tower went up was a narrow gate that likewise led directly into the courtyard. He hurried through this and across the cobblestones to the gates, swung the big crossbar out of the clamps that held it in place, and opened both halves of the gateway, swinging each one heavily back and fixing it against the inside wall. There seemed to be nobody around at all. Blight pulled the car across the road and into the middle of the yard, turned off the engine and got out.

"Look over here." Crispin had crossed to the front door and pulled the mat aside. There, carved into the massive paving stone, was the single word *HARKLINDEN.*

"Within the fire across the Stone of Harklinden," he recited. "This *must* be the Stone, and the fireplace is just inside the house, '*across* the Stone.'"

"That's it. Crispin, you must be right."

"I hope so, more than anything. If not, I've failed the quest." He replaced the mat and tried the door. The door was almost never locked, even at night, but now he found it shut fast. "They can't have gone away without me," he said. Blight held his tongue, not wishing to point out the obvious, that the boy himself had been away for going on two days, and without permission, too.

Crispin hammered with the knocker, then stepped back and looked up at the windows. They were all tightly shut. He went back to the door.

Next to it was a knob attached to a wire and spring that rang a bell inside, over the door. He gave the knob a mighty pull and the bell jangled and rang, but empty was the sound it made.

"Do you have a key?"

"I never needed one. And anyway, I'm probably too young." Again he thundered on the door with the knocker, said, "Oh come on, come on," and turned to Blight. "What can we do? We have to get inside. And what's happened to my family?"

"There's frequently an extra key kept somewhere, in case. Did you ever hear of one?" Blight felt along the shutters next to the door, but there was nothing. A curling wrought-iron light leaned out above the door but no key lay concealed in its curlicues. Crispin went back to the car and sat down on the running-board with his head in his hands.

"Come on, Crispin, what about the other doors? It's too late to give up."

"I'm *not* giving up; I'm trying to think what I've heard when I wasn't paying any attention."

"How many doors are there?"

"There's the tower door. Let's give that a try."

He ran to the narrow gate in the angle of the wall by the shed and passed back through. Blight followed. The tower door was also locked, but it had narrow glass panels let into it and Crispin rapped on these and peered through, cupping his hands to keep out the sunlight. It was no use; he could not see beyond the central core around which the stairs ascended.

"Where *can* they have got to?" he muttered to himself, and, as Blight came up, "If they had just gone for the day, Yettie would be here, getting dinner." He ran off along the terrace to try the door into the pantry, and then the French windows into the dining room. Not all of these were always securely fastened, but this time they were. Again he tried peering in through the windows; however, what he mostly saw was his own reflection. He turned back towards the tower with a feeling of hopelessness beginning to coil in his stomach. Should he break a window and reach inside? He was only seven, going on eight, and not a housebreaker, but his instincts were correct. Then a shout from Blight sent him scampering back down the length of the house and around the corner to where Blight stood, elatedly holding up a key.

"Stupid me! It was right where we keep our own—in the flower pot." He passed the key to Crispin who inserted it in the lock (It fit!) and tried turning it one way, but nothing moved. He tried the other way, but that did not work either.

"Do you think it could be rusty inside? Maybe I'm not strong enough." That was a suggestion he did not like making but he thought he would say it before Blight did. But Blight would never have said it. Tarquin would, but not Blight.

"Hold it." Blight took hold of the knob and pulled it gently toward them. "Now try."

Holding his breath, the boy tried again. The key turned, the lock rasped and clicked, the door opened. "Oh! Bravo Blight!" and he led the way into the slate passageway.

While he was still outside there had been hope; the familiar house looked as though it could still contain life and surprises. One of the things that made the house look so familiar and comforting was that he *knew* what life was like *in*side. For seven and a half years he had lived in it, explored it, played, ate, and slept in it, loved his parents, his brothers (even Tarquin), and Yettie, too, and so had grown to love the house. Now, inside, everything was different. No longer was there that woody tick-tock from the clock in the kitchen; coats and jackets still hung in the entryway but life had gone out of them. The pantry door was closed; the dining room door open. By this time the table would have been set for dinner, but there was nothing on the table. He left his companion and hurried from room to room, throwing open doors, looking into corners, turning on lights even, and then turning them off again. The house was empty. His heart sank lower and lower—empty!—and turned cold.

He met Blight again, standing at the foot of the oak stairs, gazing up into a light already beginning to lose its strength. The house was so quiet that they automatically lowered their voices to a stealthy whisper.

"Where do you suppose they've gone?" Blight asked.

"I don't know. Do you suppose they can be out looking for me?"

"If that were the case, I think they would have left somebody home. In case you showed up unexpectedly . . . . which you have."

The boy looked up once more; he tried to swallow the lump in his throat; then he shouted, "Is there anybody there?"

The works in the looming hall clock whirred and clicked, and the clock chimed the quarters, and then, in altered tone, struck the hour: seven.

"Oh good Lord, Crispin: the broom! Where is it?"

But the boy had paid no attention to the clock. He stood looking up the stairs and listening with all his heart. Suddenly, without warning, he had become a small boy without a family. Although he stood still, his mind circled and circled around the questions, "Where could they have gone? Without me? And why?

"Crispin, the broom?"

"I don't think it matters anymore. I don't know where . . . *Where . . . is . . . my family?*"

Blight knelt down on one knee and took the boy by both shoulders. "Of course it matters. It is *your* quest, and there is still time to achieve it. *Do* that. Then if there has to be another quest for your family, you and I will do it together. You, and I and Malgrin and Greyfell too; and the Pierce Arrow. I promise."

Crispin cleared his eyes with the backs of his hands and looked steadily back at Blight. "Right," he said. "In here," and led the way into the library. "Here, look." He pulled the hearth broom out of its corner and handed it to Blight.

"By heaven, Crispin, you must be right. It looks old enough; the handle is certainly pine . . ."

"And it looks like the other one, the one the witch had, as near as I can remember."

"You've *got* to be right. And it's worth more than a try. Let's go!" and he started for the door.

"Blight, wait! Do you think the umbrella may still be here? In my room? Or . . . somewhere?"

"Big help if it is. Lead the way." Crispin hurried up the big stairs and down the hallway, followed by Blight with the broom. The door of his room was unlocked and open, letting light into the hall. He went in. There on his bed, furled and snapped, lay the umbrella. He half expected that there would be a note with the umbrella, maybe from Tarquin saying where they had gone. But there was none.

"It's here. Look." And he turned to his companion who smiled a wide grin and Crispin, his excitement building, started to laugh. He felt his hope returning in a great surge and became quite giddy.

"Now Crispin, let's do this carefully. Here is the broom. Now, you want to leave the umbrella behind so that I can use it. Otherwise I might not get there until after sundown."

"Yes, I am well-reminded." And he opened the umbrella until it clicked, held it over his head, and took the broom in his left hand. "Can we both go? Or do we have to use it one at a time?"

"I don't know. We'd better stick to what we're sure of."

"Right. Please, to my—wait! The sandwiches! I'll be right back."

Handing the umbrella to Blight, he ran down the hall and down the big stairs so fast that he almost lost his balance and pitched forward. The front door was still locked but the key was in it. He flicked the safety catch and tried the key, but he had to put his shoulder to the door and push before the key would turn. He opened the door, dashed to the car, and plunged his hands into his knapsack. Out came the final two sandwiches, the peanut butter and jelly that he had been saving. Where to put them? There was nothing for it but to jam them into his pockets. He tried one in the back pocket but it was too wide so he had to use both the side pockets. How this would hinder tree-climbing he was in too big a hurry to think.

Back through the front door which he gave a shove as he passed and heard it slam behind him. Up the stairs and back down the hall to his room where Blight was waiting with the open umbrella.

"I take it these sandwiches are somehow crucial to the quest?"

"I think so. I'm almost certain they will be."

"Have you got *every*thing now?" asked Blight, handing Crispin the broom and then the open umbrella.

"Yes. I *hope* so." The boy paused for a moment, collecting himself as deeply as possible and spreading his memory as wide as possible, but he discovered nothing that he had forgotten.

"Now please, to my tree in the forest."

He was gone. The umbrella remained suspended in mid-air for a split-second, and Blight took it before it fell.

TWENTY

GREAT TREE-CLIMBING

Everything that looked green before now looked brown. It was the first thing he noticed as he materialized beneath the great tree.

"Crispin! Not a moment too soon!" This was Greyfell, who had been standing only two paces from where the boy appeared. "And you have the broom!" He put a paw up and patted Crispin's shoulder vigorously. "Good man. But quick now, the sun is beginning to—hey!"

Blight had materialized practically where the wolf was standing, jostling him aside in the process, He had the umbrella with him.

By this time the boy had noticed his mother and father standing on the other side of the great circular platform. His mother was holding baby Justin in her arms and his father had one hand resting on Tarquin's shoulder. They were regarding him with evident pride. Crispin could not move for fear his knees would give way and his heart was beating so that he could feel it in his fingertips.

The boy was so shocked by the presence of his family that he failed to notice that Frederick Riverford had yet to arrive.

"You had better start your climb, son" his father called, "the light is going."

He was right. The bottom of the tree was already in shadow. Even as Crispin glanced up he thought he could see the tide of darkness rising and he wondered whether he would ever be able to catch up with the light.

"Let me give you a leg up as I did the first time," said Greyfell, standing in the same place and making a cup with his paws. The boy grasped the broom firmly in one hand, put his right foot into the cup and steadied himself on the wolf's shoulder as he rose toward the lowest branch. The broom was even more unwieldy than the umbrella had been. Furthermore, the process was complicated because he was trying not to squash the sandwiches in his pockets, but with an extra lift and shove from Greyfell, he managed to swing up onto the branch, get onto his feet and balance his way up the gentle slope to the trunk.

"Climb carefully," he heard his mother call, and, "Excelsior!" shouted Tarquin, who had learned the word from his younger brother. Crispin couldn't begin to imagine what they were doing there and how they got there. He put the questions firmly out of his mind to concentrate on climbing as quickly and safely as he could possibly manage.

Up he went towards the light, from one big branch to another. He often wished the broom had a crook at one end like the umbrella, and then he could hang it over a branch while he used both hands to climb. Nevertheless he managed. But it was not only the broom that slowed him down, he had to keep circling the massive tree trunk to make sure he did not miss the opening for the broom handle. He hoped he would find it quickly. He did not. Of knot holes there were one or two but when he put in the broom handle nothing happened. So he climbed on. He could tell, even without looking up, that he was gaining on the light.

*

A low, angry snarl came from just above him.

"Is that my leopard? I was wondering where I would run into you again." He glanced up and saw the sleek, spotted head leaning down towards him with teeth bared.

"It's the same branch," she snarled again, "and this time you cannot pass. I have been sent here especially to make sure you don't."

"Avaunt! I am wearing the great Ring of Harklinden," the boy exclaimed, fishing it out of his shirt and holding it up on the golden chain.

"I don't care a gumdrop for what you are wearing. It's what you are *carrying* that interests me. Go ahead, make me an offer," and she stretched out on the branch with her chin supported by one paw.

"But I *am* prepared with an offer."

"How can that be? You're not even wearing your knapsack."

"Do you think I have forgotten my promise? I have a peanut butter and jelly sandwich right here in my pocket." Crispin laid the broom carefully over two branches so that it would not up-end. Then he began, very delicately, to extract one of the packets from his pocket.

"One sandwich! Do you think I can disobey the Master for *one* sandwich?"

"Ah, but I have *two* sandwiches."

There was a pause from above; a long pause.

"Both sandwiches are peanut butter and jelly?"

"Of course." He took out the other sandwich and unwrapped them both carefully, laying them on the branch in front of him. By this time the jelly had soaked through the bread and gotten onto the wax paper. He held up a piece of paper so that the leopard could lick off the jelly.

"Done!" she cried. "The bargain struck. Advance up the tree. Just leave those sandwiches right where they are. What *will* the Master say? I don't think I care. He will only turn me back into stone, so what does it matter?"

"Isn't there something I can do to help?" asked Crispin, climbing up onto the leopard's branch and reaching to scratch her head and behind her ears.

"You had best keep moving up this tree and complete your quest. That might help more than anything."

The boy climbed steadily upward but turned again, a few branches further up, to say, "I will give you a name on my way back down, if you are still here. Will *that* help?"

But there was no answer from below so he climbed on. Then, just as he was reaching the sunlight, he began to hear the galloping of a horse's hooves. "That must be Frederick Riverford on Vortex," he thought, "coming like storm clouds." He climbed steadily on, hoping that the group assembling at the base of the tree would not be disappointed in him.

*

At last Crispin reached the very branch where he had stopped climbing on his first expedition to the tree. Up here the sunlight was still bright but the shadows crept steadily upward. Yet again the empty feeling widened in the pit of his stomach and tremors ran from the back of his knees down his calves. He sat there briefly, holding on to the broomstick, with both arms clasped about the trunk of the tree. It made no difference; if necessary he would climb on until his head stuck out above the tree top. Fortunately, his mother and father could not see him from below. Above him Malgrin sat on the dead limb.

"You haven't found it?" Malgrin asked.

"No."

"I didn't think so. I have flown branch to branch, up and down this tree and have seen nothing that looked likely. Nor above here: meaning to be helpful, rather than discouraging."

"Well, I'm afraid you'll have to move. This is my quest and I will carry it out to the end, the top."

Crispin pulled his feet up onto the limb he was sitting on and gradually, holding tight to broom and trunk, he eased himself into an upright position. The sunlight was fading and his feet were already just in shadow. The dead limb was just above chest height so he could just get his elbow and arm over it for leverage. He did that and rose onto his tiptoes. Then he gently put his weight onto his shoulder and the arm over the dead branch. *Crrraaccck* went the branch, and it pulled slowly away from the trunk and then dropped onto some branches below. The boy still had his left arm around the trunk with the broom held tightly in his left hand and he hadn't lifted his toes from the branch he was on. But where a moment ago there had been the security of a branch in front of him, (although the branch was dead), there was now nothing but empty space and the darkening forest and the landscape beyond. The shadows had reached his waist.

When the limb broke and dropped off Crispin had tightened his left arm even more and brought his right arm around the trunk too. And he had shut his eyes as all the winds of the world seemed to blow through the open gap where his stomach had been. Finally he opened his eyes. Without that limb he could not climb to the top of the tree unless he shinnied up the trunk to the next limb, a maneuver he could not bring himself to think of at the moment. He glanced at the place where the branch had been and saw that it had left a hole in the trunk. On the other side of the trunk he switched the broomstick from his left hand to his right and just as the shadow slid up the trunk, he thrust the handle into the hole.

The entire tree began to quiver and tremble. Crispin, hanging on for dear life, was afraid he would be shaken off his perch. But the broomstick began to throb and grow and shoot out into branches and twigs and the broomstraws at the end turned wonderfully dark green and splayed out into clusters of brilliant pine needles. Meanwhile, the entire tree seemed to straighten its back and grow two or three full inches taller. The silvery-grey sheen of its bark disappeared at a stroke, replaced by the glinted black darkness of vigorous youth.

"Done, done, done!" called Malgrin from above. "You've done it! O Crispin, I wish I could give you wings so that you could see your whole tree at once. How glorious it is!"

But the boy had his cheek pressed to the tree bark and big tears of relief, pleasure, and pride rolled down.

TWENTY ONE

ACHIEVED

Crispin sat on the branch and watched the twilight deepen over his world. He thought he would build a platform up here and move in. Then he remembered his parents and brothers standing below and he began to climb down, nimbly, with both hands for a change, and a heart so light he felt it might float out through his mouth or the top of his head.

When he reached her branch, the leopard was gone and so were the sandwiches. But the wax papers were still there because the leopard had carefully licked all the jelly off them, leaving them pressed to the branch. He folded them and put them in his pocket. Should he call the leopard *Dauphine?*, he wondered.

Then he heard a new sound, singing . . . a broad anthem with shifting harmonies and a stately melody: but from which direction? He had circled the tree so many times on his way down, first in one direction, then in the other, that he had lost track of which way was what. He stopped and looked out to regain his sense of where things were. The singing grew from the direction of the Abbey, he thought. Moreover, there were lights—torches! It was a torch-light procession winding its way toward the great tree along the path he had taken with Greyfell and Malgrin the day before. He had not much further to climb down when the torches flowed up the steps onto the platform and now he could see they were carried by hooded figures in long robes. The Monks of Harklinden! They spread out in a great circle around the perimeter of the platform, singing the concluding joyous verse at top volume. Then there was silence, and Crispin dropped from the lowest branch into the mysteriously splendid circle of fire.

"The Ban, the Ban, you have lifted the Ban at last!" The shout went up in unison from fifty throats, and the torches blazed even more brightly out of sympathy, or so it seemed.

When the boy landed he had rolled over and come to his feet again. He discovered that he was standing in front of a tall figure robed in a habit of deep charcoal purple with hood and sleeves lined with the color of burnt oranges. Over his shoulders he wore an elaborate gold chain of office with a great round seal hanging from it. The seal was a more complicated version of the one on Crispin's ring.

Looking up he saw a face that reminded him very much of Frederick Riverford and, astonishingly, somehow or other, of his mother as well. It was the eyes that did it, a look that he could only meet with complete honesty. But the voice that spoke was gentleness itself.

"You are wearing the Ring of Harklinden, I believe. May I see it?"

Crispin slipped the chain over his head and put the Ring into the waiting hand.

"Yes, this is it, at last regained."

He struck the Ring against his own seal and immediately a most musical, bell-like note reverberated through the entire circle and was answered and echoed by the forest itself. The Monks of Harklinden emitted a deep, grateful, satisfied sigh. He put the chain around the boy's neck again.

"Wear it always," he said, "and never, under any circumstances, give it away until you yourself become Abbot of Harklinden. With it you will be able to understand the language of animals regardless of place or time. You have lifted the Ban placed on the Abbey and the forest centuries ago by the machinations of my brother. According to his plot, the Ban could only be lifted by someone seven years old who did not know that he was doing it. The Leopard of Tryce," he raised his voice, "is in attendance here? Come forward, brother."

Crispin automatically shrank backward. He felt an icy shiver run down his spine, and he felt the approach of Archduke Axel and his two henchmen. Then he grasped the Ring in his right had and stood his ground, even though the Leopard made a menacing gesture as he passed.

"That is enough of that," said the Abbot in a stern voice. "You have finished forever with threats, all three of you."

"So says the Grey Wolf of Harklinden, but how easily it could all have been different were it not for this *runt* here." And he gave the boy a malevolent look but with eyes that no longer stabbed with baleful light.

"Kneel down, Axel, and take your punishment like the man you never grew up to be. For your sake I hope that your punishment will be only that of a boy."

Archduke Axel, the Leopard of Tryce, knelt before his brother, the Abbot Blaise, and bowed his head as one who never had to bow it before. His two henchmen did likewise. The Abbot raised his hand and made the sign of the cross over their heads and they vanished. Again the monks sighed with satisfaction; even the great tree and the forest around it seemed to sigh with approval and relief.

Crispin wanted very much to turn and search out his mother and father, yet he could not take his attention from the figure in front of him. He sensed that the time for family reunion had not yet arrived.

"Blight, Malgrin, and Greyfell," commanded the Abbot, the stern tone gone from his voice.

The falcon darted to his branch, the grey wolf lay down at the feet of the Abbot, putting his nose between his front paws. Blight knelt on one knee.

"Malgrin and Greyfell, you and your families have been more than loyal, you have been tenacious. Unfortunately, there is nothing I can *do* for you except wish you long and happy lives. However, on behalf of my brothers, I *can* thank you. We are deeply and (I hope) eternally grateful."

Amen sang the monks in broad harmony, the final note dying out only minutes later.

"For you, Blight, I *can* do something, if you wish it. I can designate you Prior of Harklinden and of Priorfields, where your family will continue to hold sway for as long as they persevere."

Blight lowered his other knee and looked up with eyes sparkling and full. "It is what I have always longed for and hoped for. Thank you."

"No, we thank you." Once again the monks sang *Amen*. The Abbot reached beneath his robe and pulled out an iron ring with several keys attached. He asked Blight to stand and gave them into his hands saying, "These keys unlock; it is my hope that you never have to use them to lock."

Then the Abbot turned back to the boy. "Crispin, bring me your family."

Released like a bee from a bottle, he ran toward his parents and giving a mighty bound threw one arm around his father's neck and one around his mother's. Baby Justin would certainly have been obliterated but his mother, seeing what was coming, had passed him to Tarquin to hold. Now she took the baby back in her arms and the family walked toward the Abbot, who advanced to meet them. He had put his hood back and Crispin was even more struck by the resemblance to his mother.

"Austin and Margaret," he said, placing a hand on the shoulder of each, "so far you have done well and wisely (*Amen* sang the monks again.), shrewdly, one might almost say." Here he glanced at the boy's mother with gentle irony. "Continue in that vein and be assured of our concern and our prayers. (*Amen*.) And Margaret, since your brother has other plans, you and your sons are the only ones to carry on the line." Then he said, "Now Tarquin, I give you a sacred trust: you must look after and support your younger brother, above all patiently. Make sure he learns to do things as well as read; physical things. He will begin to grow soon and you may find yourself hard-pressed: my blessing, *our* blessing on you all."

He extended his hands and made the sign of the cross and the monks sang *Amen*.

"Finally: Frederick Riverford."

Frederick dropped the reigns of Vortex, advanced slowly and knelt down on one knee before Abbot Blaise.

"Frederick, your branch of the family has kept the ford longer and better than mine has kept the forest and the Abbey. It is time for me to place this on sounder shoulders than my own."

He reached up and lifted the chain over his head and stood with it suspended over the bowed head of the man before him. "You have long prepared yourself for this, just in case . . . You have long been worthy of it. With the consent and approbation of my brothers in Christ, I confirm you Abbot of Our Lady of Harklinden, twenty-first in that line. (*Amen. Alleluia.*) You will find everything just as it was the day the Ban fell . . . . except there are no monks. The library is intact; there is even food in the larder (it won't keep long) and holy water in the stoups. The bridges will remain for all to use who wish to gain access. I have done what I can, used my powers to counteract the greed and malice of my brother. We leave it to you to restore Harklinden to its former glory. And, oh yes: teach Crispin to ride your horse."